35

Beware of Caesar

SOME BOOKS BY VINCENT SHEEAN

Lead, Kindly Light: Gandhi and the Way to Peace
Rage of the Soul
Lily
First and Last Love
Orpheus at Eighty
Nehru: The Years of Power

VINCENT SHEEAN

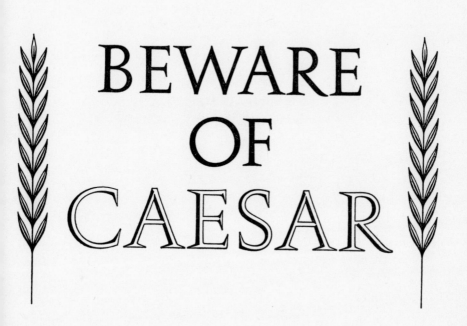

BEWARE
OF
CAESAR

Random House   New York

Beware of Caesar

I

CAESAR TURNED, lifted his golden head as high as it would go, and said: "You are here."

The man dutifully said: "Hail, Caesar."

He had said it before, but it did not count because he had not yet been noticed.

"You are very kind to have come so far to see me," Caesar said. Then he added, as if to emphasize the great kindness done to him: "So far."

"It is not very far," the old man said.

"From one of your villas in the Sabine Hills to one of your villas in the Campania cannot be very far, I suppose."

"The villas and the country houses and all the houses are yours, Caesar."

"Not," said Caesar carelessly, "not by what they tell me."

"All were your gifts and all return to you when you will."

Caesar had not yet looked the old man in the face. It would have required a different kind of effort from that of simply raising his head: that he could do, and look elsewhere, but he could not look straight up into those cold gray eyes.

Now he looked at the stone parapet against which he was standing. He was dressed in women's robes of silk in various shades, which concealed his protuberances both anterior and posterior; this was not why he wore them.

"We might sit on the parapet, I suppose," he said.

The slaves who surrounded them instantly brought forward two vast chairs with silk and gold in their cushions.

"It seems we are not so poorly provided," said Caesar. "You could scarcely do better yourself in one of your princely abodes, I think."

They sat. In this position, facing each other across a brief expanse of soft, heavy carpet from Asia, with the stone wall and the sweep of landscape to the west of them, they were much more on a level than before. Caesar was able to see into the very face, emaciated and anxious, of his preceptor. He took one straight look at the cold gray eyes and then addressed himself to the enterprise of arranging his silken robes over his fat little knees. The touch of silk seldom failed to give him pleasure, faint or keen depending on how much attention he was able to spare to it, but it was a voluptuary source in some degree, and perhaps not least because by law and custom it was reserved for women.

"Speak!" he commanded in a voice to which the silence had contributed an element of uncertainty. In spite of all the care he gave it, under the costliest obtainable instruction, his voice would rarely emerge with the tone he intended: by and large it was husky, but sometimes it squeaked, and this time it squeaked.

"Master of the World," said Seneca rather wearily, "what do you want me to say?"

There fell another silence during which Caesar rubbed the silk on his knees until his fingers were hot from it. A so-called singing bird from Africa or Asia, one of those with whom the plumage is lovelier than the song, emitted a few raucous notes and Caesar screamed in fury. The bird was silenced instantly somewhere behind them by one of the many slaves attending in the lemon grove. Seneca closed his eyes: he was thinking of the bird, the helpless bird, dying the useless but endless death, the death of a bird, of a bird only.

Caesar grew calmer and bolder. Up to now they had spoken in their native Latin. Now he fell into Greek, the most faultless, the most elegant, the most elaborately studied, and although it was very nearly as native as Latin to them, he was able to make it seem difficult, in itself an achievement, as if he danced on a tightrope for the admiration of the multitude.

"Aesthetically you abandon me," he said. "You did so long ago. No doubt you encouraged my earliest steps in poetry. I am willing to recognize this, up to a point, but if you had not done so I should have found my own way. What you do not acknowledge and will never really acknowledge is the reality and the potency of my aesthetic being. I am, as you say, master of the world. I am what the Divine Augustus called prince, the first of the Romans. But

) 5 (

that has always been the most you could see in me, and that is only a part of the whole. I am a poet, a singer, an actor, I have written words which will endure forever, and I can play the lute. Judges of merit have questioned whether there ever existed, even in the Elysian Fields, a better lute player. To all of this you are deaf and blind, Seneca, not to say dumb. My aesthetic being, which is so much the best and highest in my complex structure, has scarcely existed for you. If I had not been Caesar, Emperor and Master of the World, I should have been the most adored of all public performers. That is what you cannot understand."

Seneca closed his weary eyes, the better to see the phenomenon before him. This boy's ass is too big, his belly protrudes, his arms are too short and his eyes too small; his voice is weak and unbeautiful; he postures extravagantly, like a Greek slave in a provincial festival; and nevertheless he thinks himself the pattern of talent and beauty in the theater. It was an almost unendurable absurdity for one who had hoped to make out of this—out of this little monster—the great instrument for good in the republic of mankind.

Caesar grew even more petulant.

"You do not answer," he said. "You are chilled from your journey, old man."

Seneca aroused himself a little.

"I am not chilled, Caesar," he said slowly. "October does not oppress me, and neither will December. I have not lacked appreciation for your talents on many occasions you may remember. However, I am a servant of the Roman people."

"You always say that," Caesar murmured. Then, louder: "What does it really mean?"

"What it means is that to me Caesar is always Caesar,"

Seneca replied. "I should never have left my studies for any lute player. I came into the imperial household because I hoped to serve Rome and the Republic. That you know."

"You have said it often enough," the Emperor grumbled, going back to Latin. "How many years have I heard about the Roman virtues, and the qualities of a prince, and the difference between clemency and mercy, and the rights of the Senate and the people! Do you realize, old man, that this kind of thing can be a ——bore?"

He used an extremely obscene Greek word here, which would have been unfit for our ears even if we knew what it was.

"Oh, yes, of course," Seneca went on, fully aware that by now he could not make his case any worse. "I know how tiresome it must be to hear nothing but the praise of virtue at a time when one sees so little of it. I know that lessons which go against the grain are the hardest to learn. Perhaps they never can be learned. But if I have failed in my admiration for you as lute player, Caesar, it is plainly because I have thought of you as prince. The limitation is mine, not yours. I sought a just master for all mankind, a source of true government. I came to the palace with a bright cloud of hope round my head. I should have stayed at home."

"You were no stranger to the palace, they tell me," said Caesar with an indescribably lewd grimace. The reference to adultery with an imperial lady was plain enough for Seneca to ignore it; he went on as if it had not occurred.

"I had my own work and I let it go," he said. "The mistake was clearly mine, but my purposes were not ignoble. Perhaps it is true that no philosopher belongs in a palace—any more than he belongs in the market place."

"The Forum and the Palatine are very near to each

other," Caesar said, insinuating, in his husky and unpleasant voice, a world of illicit relationships for profit. "You are very rich, are you not? Should a philosopher be rich?"

"I have received many gifts, most of them from you," Seneca went on, undisturbed; his quiet voice conveyed no emphasis. "You may take them back again at your will. I beg you to do so. Give me a stated revenue of no great amount and I shall go back to my books in a country house where nobody will see or think of me again. If there is any accusation against me with regard to my years with you— that is, if anybody can bring a case of peculation or fraud or extortion or bribery, such as we have so abundantly seen—let them bring the case and I will answer it. All that I have is Caesar's."

"Well, that's just what everybody says in a pinch," the Emperor complained, smoothing the cosmetic on his full lips. "The only thing I know about money is that I enjoy spending it. My revered uncle Gaius, whom it would be impious to call Caligula, got through the entire treasure of Tiberius in about three years. That was an achievement I could envy. What I cannot understand is how a man can start out poor and end up rich; there must be skulduggery in it. Is it true that you have many millions in cash, Annaeus?"

"There are millions held in my name," Seneca answered slowly. He knew how foolish it would be to deny it. "They are yours when you want them."

"I am not sure I want them," Caesar said. He was impatient with so much talk of a blatantly serious nature, and yet his histrionic sense could not permit a scene of such memorable significance to go unplayed. After all, this man had governed the world, though in Caesar's name, for a good few years.

"I want only to retire to my books," Seneca repeated. "That is all. You may have everything that attaches me to Rome and the Empire."

"The number of things said to me about you," Caesar brought up, as if he had suddenly remembered the circumstance, "are many. They mostly have to do with the great wealth you are supposed to have accumulated, but there are other things, too. It is said that our failure to conquer the Parthians some time ago, when Corbulo was out there —you will remember exactly: I am not a military man—it is said that you held back the legions."

"I have always preferred negotiations to war," Seneca said. "I also am not a military man."

"Well, whatever the truth may be about that matter, nobody is going to persuade me that there is any danger to the Roman Empire. I have never been to all those places they talk to me about, but nobody can give me a valid reason for going, so why should I? My father, the Deified Claudius"—at which words he gave a quick giggle—"insisted on going to Britain, and what good did that do him? Britain, Germany, Asia and Africa all put together are not worth one day of life in Rome—that is, when things are going well. I understand that my popularity has somewhat declined lately, and that this, too, is your fault."

Seneca was genuinely astonished now.

"In what way, Caesar?" he asked. "I could have no interest in a decline of this love which, so far as I know, the people constantly bear you. On the contrary. What have I done?"

"They tell me"—and since they were still speaking Latin, Caesar had no need to indicate how many "they" might be, or of what sex, or even if they were human beings (since it was all contained in the verb)—"that you have spread rumors about my household and my manners."

Seneca sat up very straight and stared at the glittering object before him: the master of mankind, with the full masque of cosmetics for the theater plastered all over his face, from which the pale blue eyes gleamed like those of a ferret from a hole in the ground. The pale, fair hair was arranged in regular tiers of improbable curls (those which occur only in the theater or in wigs), which had been painted with gold paint so many times that they were stiff as a helmet. This incomprehensible apparition had uttered some words which the philosopher, in spite of all his experience in the matter, found it impossible to digest. He repeated them.

"Your household and your manners?"

"That is what I said," Caesar whimpered. "Oh gods above, Annaeus, why must you always make me feel like a whelp?"

Seneca looked at the imperial object and looked away, over the parapet, down toward Rome. He fetched a deep sigh then, certainly from his body and perhaps also from his soul, for he had somehow kept them together in spite of his worldly life. He did not say that Caesar felt like a whelp because he was a whelp. He did not even think it. He thought that this was what they all felt—those whom one wishes to be better than they are or can be. He said: "Caesar, it is the failure of my pedagogy. If I had been a good pedagogue—"

Then he stopped because he realized that he had spoken in Greek. They had spoken in Latin ever since Caesar introduced the subject of the Empire. The supervention of Greek was a shock to Annaeus because he had not hitherto fully understood how sharply the subjects fell into the two languages of a bilingual culture: for empire, Latin, but for pedagogy, Greek. He had never thought of it before and now marveled because it was so obvious.

He went back to Latin.

"You will forgive me, Caesar," he said frigidly. "I was speaking a language in which I was not addressed."

The bundle of silk and scent which was Caesar bounced from his chair, crossed the short space of rug, and kissed Seneca on the lips. It was not at all pleasing because the cosmetics were sticky and left traces, but Seneca himself apprehended some kind of warmth of a possibly vestigial or ritualistic nature concealed beneath the ice of his reception.

The Emperor resumed his place and asked, this time in Greek: "Why is your pedagogy at fault, Annaeus?"

"Because it has failed in love. The pupil must love the teacher. There is no other way. You never loved me, even when you were twelve years old and I came back from exile to form your mind for the government of humanity."

"But—Annaeus, forgive the question—did you ever love me?"

Seneca paused, and with the very pause he knew that it was already too late—nothing he could say now would redeem the pause. This was as certain as death itself. Why not, then, be brave?

"No, I did not love you, Caesar," he said in the same monotone. Not a nerve or tendon in his thin face, not a finger of his bony hands, nothing in his aspect betrayed the immensity of the sacrifice he was now making, or that within his disciplined mind he was already measuring its domain of disaster.

Caesar made a small, angry noise in his throat.

"The truth at last," he said. "It must be strange to your palate, old man."

"I could pretend otherwise, of course," Seneca went on,

"but it was the very essence of our relationship that my love went to the Roman people, to the Roman Republic, and through them to all those other peoples who acknowledge our rule. The desire to see a just government established—and perhaps also the uncertainties attending any effort to put thought into action—must have interfered with lesser feelings, must have oppressed or done away with the human affections. I cannot say. It has been a good many years. Even so, the pedagogue has failed because the pedagogy did not contain love. There can be no learning without love. Observe that I have known this, theoretically, for the greater part of my life, but when the chance of turning theory into practice was given me, I failed as my kind have always failed. It seems that the faculties which adapt a man to practical affairs and give him some skill in them, some ability to keep them in orderly sequence, have nothing to do with thought, or with what we call thinking. That is a solitary pursuit. The other has to do with men and women—and children—in their desires and interests. Interest and desire. It is a tangled web."

"I could never admit that you have failed with me," Caesar protested. He was sincere. The very imputation of such failure was an offense to his vanity, that carapace within which he had his being. "Do you think it is nothing to have formed, in me, a poet of supreme excellence? Perhaps I did not always attend closely enough to your precepts of government, and of—well, of virtue, let it be said—but my gifts were too powerful to be resisted, and they led me toward the art I serve. You have said that you would never have left your studies for the service of a lute player—yes, yes, you did say that, or something like it, a while ago—but let me ask you this: was there ever a more popular emperor than I have been?"

"The people of Rome have loved you," Seneca conceded, "ever since you assumed the virile toga at the age of fourteen." As he said these words his cold eyes dwelt on Nero's present attire. "You will remember that occasion."

"You wrote my speech," Caesar said with a satisfied giggle, "and a——good speech it was, too." He had employed another of his complicated Greek obscenities. "It was a little over my head at the time, of course, but I have a copy by me and one of these days I will study it again. You have admitted the popularity. Will you explain it?"

"Youth, talent, some very good government for some years," said Seneca without hesitation. He could assert the good government because to a very considerable extent it had been his government. "But reason must go deeper, and you will not deny that your immediate predecessors, Gaius Caligula and the Deified Claudius, had not given great cause for love. You came as a new force, and fresh hope arose in this much-abused people. You did well. But the Roman people, as much as any other, perhaps more than all others, is changeable, Caesar."

Caesar stared haughtily. When he spoke again, it was in Latin, hard and clear.

"We have wandered," he said. "I had originally said to you, some time ago, with regard to this matter of popular feeling in Rome, that you are held responsible, justly or unjustly, for reports inimical to me, to my household and to my manners. You repeated those words after me. You know what they mean. What will you say?"

Seneca had not yet had time to take in the enormity of the accusation. Considering that Caesar's household and domestic manners were the common subject of talk from the Rhine to the Euphrates, it seemed to outrun the bounds even of malice.

"I can say, surely, that I do not understand the ground or the sense of such a charge," Seneca said. "Your household is known to the entire Roman world. You are Caesar. Everything you do is observed, everything you say is repeated. How could I influence such matters, supposing that I ever desired to do so?"

"By a word here and a word there, an indiscretion where it will do the most harm, a revelation perhaps, or merely a funny story that will make its own way afterward." Caesar was searching for explanations; by every sign he was himself dubious in the matter but had resolved—or had promised somebody—to bring it up as part of his general dissatisfaction with his old teacher. "I don't know how such things work, Annaeus," he said pettishly, kicking out one golden sandal from beneath his robe. "I cannot go outside myself to learn. But they tell me you have spread, or caused to be spread, many stories about myself and Octavia, or myself and Poppaea, which have helped to cause this public excitement."

He avoided his tutor's eye. Beyond a doubt he was repeating words provided him by Seneca's enemies, but there were two elements in the situation which made it impossible for him to do so as if he really meant it. The first was that Caesar had never at any moment disliked public talk, attention or scandal—on the contrary, he had delighted in it and had done everything possible, including a public ritual marriage with a boy, to create it. The second unsettling element was that he knew Seneca well, and without putting any exaggerated price upon his loyalty, he did not believe the old man had time for scandalmongering, or indeed much interest in it.

The one serious aspect, in Caesar's eyes, of any such lewd talk was that it seemed to have weakened or cooled, in some slight degree, that popularity which he valued so highly. It was possible, and Seneca thought probable, that nothing else really mattered to Nero at this period, but he did adore to be adored by the masses. In his vices, so numerous and blatant, there was little true passion; in his crimes there was only fear. But where the mysteries of popular favor were involved there was in him a coherent purpose and resolve: he liked nothing so much as to sing and recite before an audience, and had brought the most highly trained professional applauders from Greece to insure that his efforts were suitably cheered. Outside the theater, too, it was the mob cries and the coarse yells of the plebeians that flattered him most. He had been accustomed to them for so long that he could not imagine a time when they might be stilled.

Seneca had already been rash enough. He would have liked to be silent now, but the words and posture of Caesar demanded an answer.

"I have done nothing," he said. "If there is wild talk or agitation, it does not come from me. The Roman people, I do not know exactly why, has shown strong sympathy for Octavia on a number of occasions."

"She is going," Nero said abruptly. "She must go."

Seneca sighed again. His whole world was slipping away from him. He knew that nothing he might say would make any difference now. His pupil's marriage to Octavia had never been right and he could not blame himself for having brought it about—it was Agrippina's work—but he dreaded the results of its failure, especially the triumph of Poppaea. Octavia, the poor, pale girl, frightened of everything in her surroundings, had suffered enough: mother, father, brother had been murdered and she could hardly be in any doubt about the complicity of her cousin and husband, not perhaps in all but in many of the crimes that haunted her imagination.

"Octavia is very young," was all he could say.

"She will go, and whatever hopes have been based on her will be disappointed."

No hopes had been or would be based on Octavia: this was another example of the suspicious fear that was growing ever stronger in Nero's mind. The girl was friendless and powerless, but the Emperor could not dispel the thought that somewhere in Rome there must be evil men, his enemies, who would make use of her against him—her misfortunes, her sad beauty, her beloved brother Britannicus, who ought (many said) to be reigning today. Decidedly Octavia must go, but not the least of his reasons was that she bored him immeasurably: he could not endure her silent company, her frequent, unbidden tears.

Seneca understood, as few others were qualified to understand, how the fate of the Julian and Claudian families was stronger than the will of its members. It was stronger because the prize for which all contended was too great: the empire of the world. For this prize no crime seemed too horrendous to be at least attempted. As the two families grew steadily more commingled, their relationships more complex and oppressive, up to and including incest, and their hatred for each other more intense, there seemed to exude from them a kind of fog of evil. And in what a brief period, in what few years, had all this come about! From the Divine Augustus to now there had been hardly half a century: only three Caesars interposed between the first and the last, this Nero Ahenobarbus, as he could not suffer to be called: this final, culminating exemplar of an unlimited will to power.

"You understand my intentions, Seneca," Caesar said.

"I think I do," said the philosopher.

"When you return to your studies you can be sure you take my gratitude with you," the prince said. "You have been the virtuous preceptor and the kind friend I needed. It would have been impossible for me, at seventeen, to take command without you. Your advice has always been good and your influence will not be forgotten. I only allow you to return to your studies and your writing because that is your wish. I am quite certain that there will come times, probably often, when I must again consult you because I know the value of your words. The link between us is never to be broken."

He rose and ceremoniously embraced the philosopher, who was not for one moment deceived by these fair words.

"You are generous to me, Caesar," the old man said. "You always have been. All you have given me is still yours."

"None of that," said Nero swiftly. "Take my thanks, and enjoy your country retreat. You will hear from me before very long again. Farewell."

"Farewell, Caesar," said the philosopher tranquilly. He was supremely aware of what he had been told. His faith in the generosity or even in the justice of his pupil had long been washed away in the flood of events, and he knew what such thanks and embraces were worth. Caesar had just, in reality, dismissed him from the imperial employment. He had also clearly said that he was about to divorce his neglected and humiliated wife in order to marry (beyond any doubt) that blazing ornament of the world's whoredom, the lovely Poppaea with the prosperous bosom. The intentions of the master were as plain to Seneca as if they had been honestly stated, and, what is more, in credit to Caesar's cunning if not to his heart, Seneca conceded that the Emperor knew it. The long years had taught them both a great deal about each other—if not, unfortunately, anything else. And at the end of the road, long or short, there could be only death, as there had been death for all the others. A man who could order the murder of his own mother would never hesitate to anticipate the end of an outworn philosopher.

So Seneca walked slowly through the lemon grove, attended by Caesar's slaves, until he reached a marble atrium at one side of the palace where his own slaves were waiting with his litter. He took his place wearily and they lifted the litter into the air on stalwart shoulders. There were four of them, with four others to assume the burden by turns; there was also an armed guard waiting outside, a score of men to surround the litter and give it consequence along the road. These appanages of power—he wondered how long they would last—could seem not much better than deliberate mockery after what he had heard.

He closed his eyes to the extravagant marble balustrades and fountains and forests of Caesar's villa. It was no worse than a dozen others, all of them produced by a frantic desire for change, for novelty in display, for an ostentation which in each case might outdo the other and in any case was unneeded for the master of mankind. Seneca could remember having seen, as a child, the mansions of the Divine Augustus: all massive dignity without any of this profusion. Even Tiberius, so long as he lived in Rome, had not squandered the Republic's money on marble, gold and fountains in such quantity. He had, instead, piled up a great treasure out of his long reign: a treasure to be thrown away in three years of madness by his nephew-grandson Caligula. There seemed no hope for this accursed house.

) 18 (

But Seneca himself was not pure; he was never untouched by the madness of his time; he had to remind himself of this constantly to avoid falling into the delusion of being better than others. No doubt, if virtue were relative instead of absolute, he might say that he had always been more pledged to rectitude than most Romans, and yet he could well remember occasions on which the pledge had faltered. He had been susceptible to the wealth that comes with power, and in his earlier years he had by no means refused himself the pleasures of the flesh. How could he condemn others? He should begin with the condemnation of himself. He was streaked and torn by contradictions. How could a philosopher of the Stoic persuasion, a follower of Zeno, a man of thought and letters, ever have yielded to the greed and luxury of this court? He was no better than Nero; he was simply older and more intelligent. The extremities of vice, as Nero imagined them and put them into action, had never tempted him, but in all probability he had more truly enjoyed his own sensual pleasures for the very fact that they were chosen, isolated and, so far as anything could be in Rome, secret. The profuse and common orgy in which Nero delighted, involving numerous participants and often spectators, aroused Seneca's distaste, but not, he reflected, on strictly moral grounds: what repelled him was the extravagation of vice, not its essence, which, like most Romans of a profoundly corrupt society, he took to be indispensable in the universe.

He drowsed a little with the gentle motion of the *lettiga* and was half asleep when a thought, unwanted and unexpected, woke him up like the ringing of a bell. It was this: Nero's base cruelty and ingratitude, his many murders, his extortion of cash and estates from the Roman nobles on almost any pretext and on the flimsiest accusations, his avid seizure of legacies and gifts, his injustice in appointments, all had borne heavily on the great families of Rome, even though the mob (gratified by gifts and favors) still cheered him. Among these great families there must be some men brave enough to take arms—?

No sooner had the thought made itself definite in his mind, sharp in outline and heavy in content, than Seneca pushed it away. Such thoughts were not for him: he was too old, he was a man of peace, and he had served Caesar for too long.

He was not, in fact, immensely old, but his severities of diet in recent years had cut down his vigor and drawn heavy, long lines in his face. He had enough body for the life of a scholar but hardly more. He was sixty-eight and was aware that he looked ten years older. He was accustomed to being called old, and not only by Caesar. If there were men rash enough to oppose Caesar, Seneca must, he thought, have nothing to do with them and must be on guard against their approaches if, now—after today's distinct farewell—they should think the time had come for such a move. Only thus could he earn a year or two of tranquillity in retirement.

He had three hours' journey altogether, half of it on a semi-rustic road connecting the Via Flaminia with the Via Salaria. It was slow and not smooth, in spite of the careful tread of the slaves. Seneca, who had tried hard to mitigate the conditions of slavery in Rome, took the institution itself for granted: he did not now, for instance, concern himself over the exertions of those who carried him. He was again half asleep when his litter and its escort came out on the Via Salaria and turned up toward the Sabine Hills. In another hour he would reach his own villa where his wife

Paulina, aware in her depths of what today's journey might or must mean, would be waiting, but without question or comment: it would be for him to speak when the time came, on the terrace in the autumn sunset or later on under the cold October stars, and tell her, in some fashion or other, that this was a destination and an end.

THE FIFTH EMPEROR was the only one who united the blood of the two clans, Julian and Claudian, which had ruled Rome since the time of the great dictator. The Divine Augustus himself, founder of the Empire, was Julian only through his grandmother, Caesar's sister, and through the dictator's favor he took the name of Gaius Caesar and was thus adopted. Having no sons, Augustus himself was obliged to have recourse to adoption. His wife Livia, by her first marriage to Claudius Nero, had two sons, of which the elder, Tiberius, was raised to the purple when Augustus died, and was succeeded, after a reign of twenty-three years, first by his grandnephew Gaius Caligula and then by his nephew Claudius. All of these three, Tiberius, Caligula and Claudius, were Claudian by blood and Julian only by adoption.

Nero had, on his mother's side, direct descent from Caesar Augustus: his mother Agrippina, daughter of Germanicus and sister of Caligula, was, through her own mother the elder Agrippina, granddaughter to Julia and thus great-granddaughter to Augustus. The laws and the customs of Rome did not admit the female line to constitute inheritance (except by testament) and least of all would it have been possible for a woman to be Imperator, or commander of the forces; yet there is no doubt that Nero gained a great deal, in his youthful advance to the throne, by the fact that his ancestry on one side led straight to Augustus and thus, by Roman law, to Caesar the Dictator.

Adoption and intermarriage had so befogged the outlines of the Julian-Claudian house that the genealogy was no longer distinct, and it was difficult to know whether, when a prince of this house said "my father," he meant his real father or some other relative (uncle or cousin) who had adopted him. Gaius Caligula adopted his own brother Tiberius, and (up to the moment when he felt it necessary to kill him) always referred to the young man as his "son." The writers who chronicled these relationships were no more secure in their details than the members of the imperial brood, and a loose, unformulated belief in some kind of general Caesarean family, more inextricably linked together than others, partly divine and wholly outside the law, grew up among the Romans. The worship of certain individuals who had been consecrated as divine in life (as were Augustus and his wife Livia, in the style Augusta) was important in the ritual; others who had been deified after death, such as Julius the Dictator and Claudius the Fourth Emperor, was less solemnly fixed in the pantheon. Indeed, the deification of poor old Claudius, which Agrippina felt she owed as compensation for having murdered him, was treated with irony and contempt even at the time. To ensure the throne to her young son Nero (and thus the power to herself, or so she thought) was the only purpose of Agrippina's life; she would have deified a household donkey, as her brother Caligula made his favorite horse a Senator, if by so doing she could gain power.

Nero, the culmination of all the Julian-Claudian epos, had been taught from childhood to esteem his mother's ancestry above that of his real father, Ahenobarbus; and after Agrippina, in pursuit of her ambitions, had married her uncle Claudius and obliged him to adopt her son, he received the name of Nero (a Claudian name) and accounted it an insult if anybody thereafter called him Ahenobarbus. His "brother" Britannicus (in reality his cousin), the only son of Claudius, offended often in this respect, and owed to such things, as much as to his imperial birth and the affection of the Roman populace, Nero's hatred and revenge.

By the time he was twenty-five Nero had, precociously by any standard, committed a wide variety of crimes; none, except the murder of his mother, preyed on his mind, and that only when some natural misfortune (a storm, an earthquake) made him suffer from superstitious fears as well as those which habitually afflicted his imagination. In the impenetrable relationships of the Augustan house there was a long trail of blood from the very outset, and son, brother, sister, nephew were words compelling no loyalty and even no compassion where power was endangered, but even in that family the crime of matricide was looked upon with horror.

Thus Octavia had little reason for hope. Young, frail and timid, with no liking for public matters and no experience, she had first been taught to regard Nero as her brother and then was compelled to take him as husband, while the tyrannical Agrippina, officially her "mother" as wife of Claudius, became her mother-in-law. The young girl could have saved herself if, by any chance, the prince had found her appealing to his sensuality, but, in her youth and terror, her *pudor* as the people called it, she quelled his desire before it could even be aroused, and he openly spoke of her, even from the beginning, as "cold" and repellent to him. He had numerous other diversions with both sexes, and to her relief she was saved from his love even though it was by his hate. She became in practice a prisoner, surrounded by spies as well as jailers, and after the murder of her brother Britannicus she felt herself alone in the world. No comfort was to be found in the support of her cousin, mother and mother-in-law Agrippina, who had only smiled upon Britannicus and Octavia as another means of exercising power; but then Agrippina, too, was put to death, and there was no curb except, perhaps, the words of the ageing Seneca, upon the will of the prince and Emperor.

And yet there was something in this pale, fragile girl which aroused powerful sympathies among both the nobles and the people of Rome. She was violently cheered in the public processions and her statues were wreathed with flowers. Her many misfortunes, in particular the poisoning of her beloved brother Britannicus at Caesar's table, had given her virtue an aureole. Virtue was not always popular in Rome; sometimes it seemed that vice was more attractive to the masses. Nero was most beloved when he was making an exhibition of himself in the public theater or passing through the streets with a catamite in his arms: when he murdered his mother he became a hero. In spite of these anomalies, the purity of Octavia's character, a quality unfashionable and rapidly becoming unknown, was what the Romans loved in her, perhaps for its rarity, perhaps in some nostalgia for the women of the Republic, or even perhaps because at some crucial moment she had smiled at them sweetly, with none of the arrogance they had learned to expect from the ladies of the Palatine.

A clever or ambitious girl might have made use of the sympathies she aroused. Octavia was incapable of calculating, possibly even of knowing, that her innocence had its own strange power, or that her very helplessness stirred forgotten impulses of honor in the Roman heart. She soon discovered, with astonishment and fright, that this was so, and that the people of the city cared more about her destiny than she did herself.

The Emperor waited only a day after Seneca's dismissal. He could scarcely have waited more. His official and obsessive mistress, the full-bosomed Poppaea, gave him no rest on this subject; she had long demanded her "rights" as his wife, and now that Agrippina was out of the way, safely dead and almost forgotten, with Seneca relegated to some country house in the hills, there seemed no further obstacle to her ambition.

Caesar issued the order for Octavia's retirement to a villa in the south, and at the same time he asked for a study upon grounds for divorce so that he could marry Poppaea. Once this had been done he left his retreat in the Campania and set out, with Poppaea and an immense train of slaves, servants, courtiers and guards, for the Palatine.

They arrived in Rome to find that their news had gone ahead of them—so slow and clumsy was the imperial mode of travel—and that there had been some obscure signals of discontent among the people. So far there had been no disorder, but the wreaths had piled up on the statues of Octavia during the night and there were angry groups gathering all day long in the Forum. Some of Caesar's advisers were, if not precisely afraid, at least inclined to take the situation seriously and to wonder if it might not be better for the Emperor to leave Rome again. There was actually no danger that the praetorian guard might not easily overcome, and their loyalty—owing to the lavish donatives with which Nero rewarded them—was beyond question. But to use the guard at all would mean open violence, leading, perhaps, to worse, and there was anxiety in the air.

Caesar himself did not care in the least how much bloodshed there might be, so long as it did not involve him, but he did care with petulant frenzy—the intensity of a small child in a tantrum—about his own popularity. He now found, or was informed, that the effervescence in the streets, although directed against Poppaea and in favor of Octavia, was also in part against him, even though as yet only by implication. He fretted, strutted and fumed, but there seemed little he could do, especially since Poppaea was now in the full flood of all her anger, resentment and reproach. She had upbraided him relentlessly for two or three years; it was worse now.

"Who am I," she demanded, "that I should be unworthy to be Caesar's wife? What of my rank and my ancestors? Am I unworthy by beauty or fortune? Have I not done enough to deserve the public honor? Must I have shame heaped upon me forever? What is this Octavia, who is not even your wife, who is nothing and less than nothing, except that she is Messalina's daughter and will some day be found to have Messalina's tastes? How can she stand against your real wife, and how can you permit such equivocation? Who are you, Caesar?"

"By this time," Caesar said with a pout, "I don't know who anybody is. Can't you stop talking for a while? My head aches from it."

"You were your mother's ward," Poppaea said in her calculated fury (she never changed color, lost control of her voice or in any way impaired the perfection of her features). "You were your mother's slave. You were her thing. I thought for two or three years that only Agrippina kept you from doing your duty to me. But now that you have—"

"Don't say what you are going to say!" he interrupted. "Don't say it!"

"Very well. But it is true. Agrippina is no longer here and you still hesitate. What is at the root of this behavior? That old fool Seneca, with his pompous sentences, can't be blamed now. He went—I saw him go—and he will not come back."

"You ask what ails me, but I could just as well ask what ails you," was his answer. "For almost five years now, anyhow four, you have had everything you chose to possess in this world. Nothing has been denied you. Of all the women in Rome you are the most admired, cherished, perhaps spoiled. Who has more jewels than you? Who has—"

She cut him short.

"Jewels," she said with contempt. "What are jewels? I want a crown, Caesar. A crown."

"There are no crowns in Rome," he said. "Rome is a republic."

"I know. Of course. Rome is a republic. The Roman Senate and People. The Roman Republic. Yes, indeed. Whenever you are cornered you throw those words at me. Most of the time you behave as if the Roman Senate and People did not exist, and as if the Republic were your private property, but if I claim what is my right, my undeniable right, you go back to the language of your great-grandfather. Is this your way to understand love?"

"I know love," he said, fixing his pale eyes on the ample curve of her bosom, no doubt for fear of meeting her glance.

She had one weapon which never failed to afflict him grievously.

"You took me from Otho," she said. "My brave, handsome Otho, the pattern of what a man should be. Why don't you let me go back to Otho? I don't care how far away it may be. As Otho's wife I can hold up my head with honor. Otho was a nobleman; he did not sleep with slaves and adopt their manners. Everything in his house was noble and he was himself—ah, you know what he was and is! I can go back to him and be proud as well as happy."

He fidgeted and whimpered.

"Otho is in Lusitania," he said, irrelevantly. "I have never been there. I do not know what it is like. I don't believe you know what it is like either. And anyhow I cannot allow you to leave me now. Poppaea, why can't you be patient? We must go slowly."

"I have been patient ever since you first took me from Otho," she said more quietly, observing that she had shaken his defenses (as usual) by the mere mention of that name. "I was a victim of my hopeless passion for you."

She told the shameless lie with immense effect: her eyes,

so dark and brilliant, seemed to glitter with real tears as she gazed at him.

"You seduced me," she said even more quietly; there was no way of reflecting, in her persuasive presence, how many others had performed this office before him. She had a power of histrionic suggestion, even in the movements of her hands or the tone of her voice, which made it impossible for him to doubt her while she was actually there, especially since she contrived to give even her reproaches an overtone of flattery. She turned her head away.

"Now I must go, Caesar," she said. "If I am not to be your wife I must think what to do with the rest of my unhappy existence. I cannot bear this shame forever."

"You will be my wife," he said rather wildly, looking around him to see how many of the slaves were within hearing. "I've told you often. I must go slow in this. Poppaea, do not doubt me. Go, if you must, go to your own rooms, but if you start to make any preparation for departure, any whatsoever, you realize that I will be informed immediately and I will not permit it. I will not permit it. You must trust me and believe that I will do as I say."

"If I have spoken too much," she said with swimming eyes, "it is because of my love for you, Caesar."

He turned, sharp of tongue and temper, upon those counselors who were waiting for him in the next room with reports from the city. He was angry, not with Poppaea, who retained her hypnotic spell today as yesterday, but with the circumstances which made it impossible, or at least unwise, to gratify her wishes at this moment. The rituals of marriage meant less than nothing to him but he could see that a Roman matron of the noblest blood, with a family—with two or three families—stretching out all over Italy, with a pride almost beyond measure, might see the matter in another light. He knew all about Poppaea and reproached her with nothing; all her husbands and paramours put together—he had it on her word—were obliterated from her life and mind from the moment of their first embrace. It was unjust and unfair, he thought, that she should be deprived of her "crown" (what crown?) because of that fabricated marriage with his pallid, flavorless sister Octavia. His resentment of Octavia intensified until it almost choked him.

And yet there they were, the reports from the city. An extemporaneous meeting here, another there: there was no doubt a movement afoot, organized or unorganized, to show favor to Octavia. The offerings at her statues in the city grew more numerous all afternoon. There had even been one or two public speeches, not by anybody of importance, but to mysteriously formed and mysteriously dissolved groups of fifty, eighty or a hundred citizens at a time.

Added to troubles over grain and taxes, this was a little too much for the five or six men who controlled the city. They were afraid that sooner or later some demagogue might amalgamate the grievances, and so they said. They suggested as subtly as possible that Octavia might be recalled to Rome—thus removing one part of the irritation to the people.

Caesar, in spite of his bad temper and his impatience, tried to listen to them, and did so with less difficulty than usual because in his own head was germinating an idea. He brought it forth, at last, without asking for an opinion, since it seemed to him good.

"These demonstrations are centered upon statues of Octavia, which, as is the custom in our house, are placed in public places and temples. I have the remedy. Let these statues, or some of them, be removed tonight and put into the gardens of the palace. Then let some of Poppaea, which are now standing in the gardens, be erected in the public places, in the Forum and elsewhere, the places from which Octavia's are removed. It will be impossible, in that case, for the floral offerings to go on, or if they do they will have a different sense. I have thought of this just now while you were speaking. It will be an answer, it will show that we are not afraid, and it will put a stop to this particular form of insolence. I think you will find that in a day or so everything will be quiet again. These are only whims on the part of the Roman people. I understand them. Let the orders be given for tonight."

They stared at him, for an imperceptible moment, as if they could hardly believe it: to their sober minds the notion was imbecile, a species of provocation; and yet habit took over, and they all said "Hail Caesar!" as if he had produced a luminous word or a heroic deed. They were then given leave to depart, for he had another group of counselors in another room on the faraway matters (Britain, which was giving great trouble, and Parthia, which never ceased doing so) to which he found it so difficult to attend. As he left the room to cross the atrium he perceived that his friend Tigellinus, the commander of the praetorian cohorts and partner of his most private pleasures, wanted to speak to him.

This Sophonius Tigellinus had only recently obtained his high office in Nero's favor, and was still compelled to share it with Faenius Rufus, who had other claims: the two of them together, Tigellinus for his intimacy with Caesar, Rufus for his standing with the people, were taking the place of the sturdy and upright Burrus who had guarded Nero's youth and young manhood. Seneca had relied heavily upon Burrus for many years in the guidance of the young prince; but Burrus was dead (not many on the Palatine were brave enough to ask how) and Seneca had gone to the hills. This Tigellinus was a well-grown, handsome young man with thick, hairy legs and massive arms, but a warier prince than Nero might have taken warning from his never-opened eyes, almond-shaped and shaded by long black lashes, which, through the exiguous fissure allowed them, seemed to make constant suggestions of lewdness. Tigellinus saw, with his indecent eyes, the secret parts of every person before him, and conveyed an awareness of it, so that none except the most abandoned were at ease.

"Commander," Caesar said, "speak."

He went on out into the atrium and Tigellinus followed. The other courtiers had already gone the other way.

"I am responsible for your safety in Rome," Tigellinus said, "and believe me, Lord, you are safe."

This appellation, "Lord" (*Dominus*), was servile: it was originally used by a slave to his master, and the Divine Augustus had never permitted it to be applied to himself. Nor had Tiberius, indeed: it took the madness of Gaius Caligula to encourage it among freeborn Romans. Nero liked it; in common with everything else of an abject nature, it flattered his sense of unique destiny and power. (He was perverse enough to use it upside down, too, and had been known to call a slave "Lord" in his sensual excitement.) Tigellinus was apt at all the courtly arts, and, in spite of his square-built, soldierly appearance, none could give him lessons in corruption.

"You are going to hear discussions of empire," he said in an undertone, "and they will talk chiefly of the war in Britain. But there are dangers a little nearer than that. You have sent Sulla to Gaul and Plautus to Asia. Sulla can arouse Gaul in the name of the Deified Julius. Plautus is too rich; he is the grandson of Drusus; he now has legions at his command. I am not there to watch him."

Caesar was not dressed for the theater this evening: his face was never wholly clean of cosmetic, nor his curls of gold paint, but at least he had a more natural look than he had worn for Seneca a few days ago, and his garment was the virile toga. Thus he was aided in the assumption of a little more dignity than usual. Moreover, Tigellinus paid him the great honor of being slightly shorter than he, so that there was no embarrassment on that score.

"Sulla and Plautus," he said, musing. They were the two men he feared most in Rome, because of their exalted ancestry and their public worth. Plautus was, indeed, his cousin. "We may speak of this again later. I will see you in the evening, Tigellinus, after the banquet."

He went on to his imperial duty, which did not occupy him long. They talked of Britain, indeed, and of the stubborn queen who was continuing a dangerous rebellion after her husband's death. He had already read the dispatches and resented their tone. It seemed to him—quite falsely, since no busy general desired his presence—that there was some element of reproach in the fact that he had never been to Britain, nor indeed to any of the other outposts, and that the unspoken word was, when things went badly, that a better Caesar would have commanded his own troops. Nero repudiated the notion with vehemence: what did they know, these generals, of his duties to music and poetry, to art in general? He had not the slightest intention of risking his skin in any forays among the barbarians. If he gave a victorious general a triumph, or an ovation, or even a thanksgiving, that was enough.

The reproach he imagined was ludicrous, and if he had had the slightest experience of war even he would have known it. The commander in Britain, Suetonius, would have been horrified to find an imperial court landed upon him in the midst of his desperate struggles with the Druids and the savage tribes. Among the chosen counselors at table not one would have suggested such a thing. There was talk of transferring troops from Germany to Britain, but no decision was taken, and Caesar's order was (as he had intended from the beginning) to leave everything to Suetonius.

He was thus free to get to his own rooms and change his garments for the pleasures of the evening, in which he took far more interest.

While he was so engaged, Acté came to him, sending in a slave first to ask his permission. He was in a white silken robe, very loose, of the kind men only wore during the Saturnalia, and his preparations were almost complete.

Acté stood before him silently, waiting for his word to speak. Her soft, dark eyes were tender and a little worried.

"Do you like this silk, Acté?" he asked her, turning from his looking glass. "It has just come from your own country."

She did not look at his garments but at him.

"I like the silk, Lord," she said. "But I like you better than any silk."

"I know," he said, in a voice gentler than he was accustomed to use to most people.

"That is why I am a little concerned this evening," she went on. "I have been into the city to see my friends there. There is much talk and much excitement among people, some people, not my friends but others, and the riffraff in taverns and the fishshops, too, along with some quite respectable citizens. I do not know quite who they all are, Caesar."

Her quiet voice in its most imperfect Latin always had a soothing effect upon him.

"Do not be anxious, little Acté," he said. "They are talking of Octavia, I suppose."

"Yes, Lord—and of Poppaea, too."

She lowered her eyes as if to indicate that she knew how bold it was of a slave (even a slave set free) to mention by name so grand a lady of the Roman aristocracy.

"I have been told about it," Caesar said, looking at her with some curiosity. "I have never asked you who these friends are whom you visit so often in the city," he went on, touching a gold chain at her neck; he had given it to her once and she wore it almost always. "Are they from your own country?"

"Some are from my country," she said submissively, "and with them we speak my own language. They work in the markets, and one or two were slaves but are now free."

She did not mention that she had bought their freedom with the money she had in such useless abundance, money from Caesar's many forgotten presents; nor did she say that "one or two" was a minimal account of their number. She raised her head and smiled at him.

"But there are Roman citizens among them, too," she said proudly.

"I have heard," Caesar said idly, not intending harm for this once, but pursuing the twist of his curiosity, "that they belonged to some sect or other, some division of the Jews, perhaps, or so I remember somebody telling me."

Her eyes closed as if in pain.

"Let it not worry you, little Acté," he said kindly. "All the devils of the lower world live on the Palatine, and they all bring me tales about each other and everybody else. They cannot poison me against you. You know that, don't you?"

Her eyes opened wide: radiant darkness (a darkness containing great light), they gave him some assurance he never seemed to find elsewhere. He took her hand and spoke in Greek. She was a Nabataean Arab from the Petra region but had been carried off to the Hellenic world as a child, and Greek was easier to her than Latin. She could read and write Greek and Aramaic, but Latin always was a foreign language.

"You are my faithful friend," he said in an undertone, for there were slaves everywhere in the curtains and shadows of the house, "and if it had been left to me, as it was not, I should have married you six or seven years ago. It could not be, Acté, but I will never abandon you. You know it. You will be with me whatever happens."

Her great eyes were glittering inside the dark circles she made about them.

"To the end, Caesar, to the end," she said, and kissed his hand.

They may have had different meanings for these words, she in the saying and he in the hearing, since he never really doubted (in spite of his incessant fears) that he could remain supreme. Even so, whatever they meant, the truth contained was felt by both. He was sincerely moved, as he seldom was by anything but a song.

"I am not going into the city," he resumed, again in an undertone and again in Greek. "I will watch what happens for a few days. Tonight most of the statues of Octavia will be moved from the public places. That will put a stop to one kind of show. We are not afraid, are we. Acté?"

"I am never afraid for myself. Only for you."

"Did your friends think the excitement in the city would lead to anything? To violence, for instance?"

"They thought it was serious," she said. "I feel more secure now that I realize you knew all about it. They do not tell you everything, Lord. They do not tell you even a small part of the things you ought to know about how the people speak and think or even what they need. That is why I come to you and tell you myself."

He raised his hand as a sign of dismissal; it was time for his supper, but he did not let her go without an embrace. This required some readjustment of his own appearance after she had gone, so that it was several minutes before he himself left the room. As he did so, through a curtain at the side there appeared the boy Sporus, the blue-eyed Greek, frowning fiercely. Caesar looked at him in dismay: the boy must have been there all the time.

"What's the matter now?" he inquired with a touch of his usual ill temper. "You look as if you'd swallowed poison."

"I heard her," the boy said. "I was here and I heard what she said."

"Well, what of it?" Caesar asked. "She told me something I already knew, from the city."

"I don't mean that. I don't pay any attention to that. I don't know what it means. I heard her say that she would be with you to the end, Lord."

"Indeed. She meant it and I believe her."

"Do you not believe that I also will be with you to the end? Have I not proved—"

"Yes, Sporus. You have proved your love."

He took the boy's hand and held it for a moment.

"Do not be jealous of Acté," he said. "She is your friend."

Through his misery the Greek boy looked ashamed for a moment. He knew that Acté was his friend, perhaps his only friend.

"I heard a pledge, Lord," he said, controlling his tears. "I was not included in the pledge. I should be. I have given more—more than anybody else."

"You will never be abandoned, Sporus," the Emperor said. "To the end. You and Acté will be with me, whatever happens."

The boy retired again behind the curtains, reassured for the moment, although he could not possibly know—as Caesar knew—how great was his sacrifice. The Emperor went on his way, and the slaves and guards in attendance gathered for the procession. In his mind was the thought, accompanied by a sudden ominous pang of premonition, that this might be all too true—that Sporus and Acté, Acté and Sporus, the girl slave and the boy slave, might be with him to the end when all else had fallen away and all others had betrayed him. An Arab girl and a Greek boy, caught in some military expedition beyond their comprehension or memory, had been swept across the world to this cold destiny, to be his only friends and lovers. He shook off the notion when he caught sight of the lights and flowers of the company assembled; and there, beyond the winecups, was Poppaea.

III

Fragment of a lost letter from Annaeus Seneca to his disciple Lucilius:

. . . speaking thus, he went away, and I have not seen him since.

Such matters have not usually formed the content of my epistles to you, dear Lucilius, since I have tried to make these into moral arguments which might serve the purpose of preparing your mind for the deceptions, sorrows and disappointments of the world. You know that in my opinion the wickedest and unworthiest of men are generally the happiest, the most highly rewarded, and the most certain of their own rectitude. I can hardly walk outside my door without seeing criminals of every sort who have, by vice and fraud and cruelty, obtained the esteem of the citizens and their highest offices. From this to undertaking to end such abuses—providing an end were possible—is a different matter altogether and involves the entire passage from thought to action. Since I have often urged you to abandon any kind of public office, high or low, and give yourself to reflection, you know that I would never accept, for even a moment, the thought of lending myself to plots or plans which vainly aim at changing the current of public affairs.

This man came to me with letters from old friends and I received him honorably. What he had to say to me was quite outside the limits I have set for myself. No matter what horrors befall the state, it can never be said that I did not try to avert them in my time, but I will not take part in any attempt to enforce a different moral order. First of all, I consider that it would be vain to do so. The vices we deplore and the abuses we condemn are the results of a predisposition on the part of mankind, and until we can cure the cause we shall have no luck with the effect. Second, and finally, under the present circumstances and under the proposed leaders, any effort at substantial change would cause great bloodshed and further evil to the state.

I understood little of what he told me, because my mind was abstracted and I was unfamiliar with many of the relations and situations he expected me to know. Even so, there can be no doubt in his mind that I shall have nothing whatsoever to do. . . .

. . . so that in the end, as usual, whatever you do is right. At the same time I confess that I wish you had given me more particulars of the state of public affairs in Rome. Here in Sicily we get contradictory reports and do not know what to believe, since the deepest causes of discontent, heavy taxes and the grain shortage, have recurred so often in recent years that we cannot understand what is new or grave about them. Gossip of the imperial household is more widespread than ever, and there is no real way for a magistrate to discourage it, since it is everywhere. At present it is centered upon the fate of Octavia, who is said to be the victim of a shameless persecution by the woman Poppaea. Here, as I understand is the case elsewhere, opinion is strongly opposed to Poppaea's ambition.

What cuts most deeply into my own sense of the public welfare and decorum is the list, apparently without end, of knights and noble Romans who are put to death, day after day, for crimes against the state. So much fraud, corruption, extortion and treason could hardly be contained within one city, it seems to us at this distance, even if that city is Rome.

We are left with two possible conclusions, since these charges must be either true or untrue. If they are true, then every virtue of the Roman character seems to have crumbled away all at once, and at every level of the imperial administration. This is a hard thought and one which offends our sense of what is natural or probable. But if the charges are untrue, then what monstrous persecution is this which seeks out and destroys the best men both in youth and in maturity? Your own retirement from the

Palatine was a shock to many in these regions, and although I have long known that your wishes ran in that direction, I thought that, as before, your desire to perform a duty would overcome your inclination. Only from you—and by indirection—have I understood that this was Caesar's will, not yours, even though it may coincide with yours.

Do not be alarmed at my frankness. The slave Glaucus, who brings you this, is the most faithful friend, and I am certain that he would die rather than give up a letter, which, incidentally, he carries in a manner most difficult to detect. If you wish to reply with equal frankness, keep him with you a day or so while you consider, and then answer without fear.

I am procurator of Sicily and young enough to look forward to a long career of service if I had faith in it. Your constant admonitions have induced in me a doubt of the service itself, of its usefulness and of my suitability to it. If I were to retire to the sweet gardens of philosophy, as you wish me to do, I should certainly have less property to leave to my eventual descendants, but I might lead a more complete life in my own time. I am well aware of your poetic line—is it Menander?—according to which we truly live only the smallest part of our lives.

I know that time is not life, and I know that most of what is loosely called life is really only time elapsed.

Indeed there must be few, among the many who revere you, who have more thoroughly studied the works in which you tell us what you think. *Of the Brevity of Life* and *Of the Tranquillity of the Soul*, those twin children of wisdom, are the books beside my bed always, along with others which change from time to time. I have long meditated on the words of Zeno, once strongly upheld by you:

The wise man will always intervene in the affairs of the state if circumstance does not deter him. From these you seem to have passed to other words, without loss to the tranquillity of your soul, the earlier words of Epicurus to which Zeno was making reply: *The wise man will always hold himself afar from state affairs if circumstance does not drag him into them by force.*

I do not accuse you of contradiction because the growth of the mortal mind on any one subject of thought is one of its claims to respect. My stage of growth, however, is different; I am young; my nature cannot wholly repudiate worldly ambition; the vision of eventual marriage, children, grandchildren, an estate to survive me, a position among the citizens, cannot be put away by the will alone. I do adhere to the lesser of your precepts, to keep all possible time for myself, to read and think in the hours I can preserve from public duty, and to meditate at least as much as to act. Your greater precepts, involving the retirement from all public office, are as yet beyond me. And in saying this I must remember, as a good but not always logical disciple, that in fact the office I hold was given me by your will. If I am procurator of Sicily it is because you saw fit to put me here. This is no reproach but an expression of gratitude for an opportunity which, at this stage of my being, arouses my capacity for civic virtue without withering my predilection for philosophy.

But if I am to remain here, as I think I must for the time, it would be light and sustenance for me if I were to receive some indications from you about what is actually going on in Rome. If I were in Asia, Africa or Britain, so far from Rome that no news could be fresh or relevant, it would be a different matter, but in Sicily, where we are at arm's length or within earshot, it is a source of bewilderment and anger to be so unsure. One is supposed to know and one knows nothing. This is perhaps the difficulty—and perhaps the danger. I need hardly say that I am known to be your disciple and friend, and as such am exposed to more curiosity at this moment, not to say calumny, than is usual even in the public service. Since your retirement I am looked upon with special interest as if I, too, may be expected . . .

Seneca to Lucilius, another fragment:

. . . and in my opinion the slave speaks excellent Greek. Of his loyalty, in my opinion, you have made a correct estimate.

The affairs of state do not look prosperous or promising. Remember that I am four hours from Rome, and take no part in these matters, but there are many who come and go, and of course it is only recently that I was myself heavily involved, so they are all eager to tell me what they know in the illusion that I may sooner or later return. At the moment the commander of the praetorian cohorts, Sophronius Tigellinus, is supreme, and one by one he is obliterating any possible opponent or critic of his conduct. Some of the terrible charges and condemnations which have so disturbed you are due simply to the jealous power of this evil man, who is determined not to let anybody stand against him. Some charges there are, although few, which might be sustained in any court of justice. For example, you know enough of the world to be aware that if a man is superintendent of the grain supply and is charged with making money out of it, there is a strong probability that it may be true. (The temptation is enormous and the tradition of the office is not against it.)

It is also sometimes true that a proconsul in a far province of Africa or Asia has been extortionate without our knowledge here. We normally learn of such things, where they exist, long after they have run their course. A man retires to Rome with colossal wealth; suspicion arises; and then private enmities, of course, produce public accusations. They should not; but this is the world.

Yet these justified charges and punishments are, as you truly suspect, nowhere near enough to fill out the terrible list of knights and nobles who have been put to death in the past year. Some, indeed many, are the victims of Tigellinus; some, in my view, are the victims of Poppaea; but I am willing to say to you, in utter sincerity and whatever the danger may be, that most are victims of Caesar himself. He has grown steadily more fearful of conspiracies against him, plots to assassinate him, plots to overthrow his power, almost altogether imaginary but sufficient to inflame his anger whenever there is the slightest excuse for it. A man may enrage him by having a better singing voice than his own—I do not exaggerate: it was one of the main reasons for his hatred of his brother Britannicus—and from this to being involved in a traitorous conspiracy is no step at all in his incomprehensible imagination. The frivolity of his reason bears no relation to the horror of his act. He will kill for a shadow, for the shadow of a butterfly—for the song of a bird. It is not even altogether through fear, jealousy and suspicion: it is also because he likes to kill. He actually derives a sensuous pleasure from it, because it feeds his sense of power and some other, more occult sense of which I am thankful to know nothing. Sometimes I wonder what I was doing in all those years when I had the training of his mind, or thought I had. I was unable to foresee the strength of the instincts and appetites which govern that mind.

There are times when I wonder if he has not gone mad, like his uncle Gaius, but then he displays great shrewdness, immense capacities for dissimulation and play acting, a cleverness of understanding and appealing to the lowest elements in the people, and a half dozen other qualities, not in themselves admirable at all, but together quite enough to preclude any possibility of insanity in the mind which exhibits them. The boy can deceive, almost to perfection, almost anybody, and at almost any time, even when the person deceived has every reason to know better: and this quality alone, I consider, proves him to be quite sane. His uncle Gaius could never have deceived a cat or a dog. I remember Gaius—O time! Unfortunately, I remember them all, straight back to the Divine Augustus.

Therefore, let me say to you, Lucilius, and at the peril of my life (for the good slave might come to evil on the road), this thing: if you are to remain in public service or in any way before the public, *beware of Caesar.* That is, from the practical point of view, the best advice to be given anybody in the Empire today. His eye may alight on anybody and his whim is fatal. There is no formulable *principle* of evil in him (you cannot say he obeys any principle, even of evil), but he is himself evil, and that is enough. To escape his notice might be the best fortune that could befall a public officer except that, without it, the highest rewards are impossible. I do not think you want or should have the highest rewards. I have hope yet that you will see the advantages of the garden. But if you remain in service at all, remember that I have told you after deep consideration, and at no slight risk, to remember your greatest peril: *beware of Caesar.*

Now, of course, our society is itself corrupt and evil flourishes. That has been the fact ever since I can remember. The virtues of the Roman Republic, if they ever existed, and I am conscious of no impiety in wondering, have not survived into the present. This present state was called, by the Divine Augustus who invented it, "the principate." It does not take the place of the Republic but is an administrative adjunct to it. Administrative, indeed! All the organs of the Republic remain but without function or power. Who is this prince who governs the "principate"? He is the commander of the forces, elected, acclaimed, proclaimed by the forces, and in reality perhaps only by the praetorian cohorts, humbly confirmed by the Senate and the people of Rome. In fact, for half a century this prince has been some member of the same family or nexus of families, an heir, in a sense, to Julius Caesar the Dictator. In truth, clearing away all the legal and administrative fictions, we live under a complete dictatorship, except that it has no time limit and has turned into a semi-hereditary institution. Our ancestors invented dictatorship as a defense for our liberties in time of peril. When the peril had passed the dictatorship ended and the power returned to the citizens. The dictatorship has now overwhelmed all our liberties and the Emperor, commander of the troops, has in practice every power it is possible to imagine among mortals. The Republic is a dream; the Empire, far-off and widespread, is a reality, but touches few among us; only the Emperor is real.

And what an emperor!

You know, Lucilius, that I do not like talking of the immediate affairs of men. My letters to you have always been of another character and for another purpose. If they are published, and I have always considered this desirable, they will be called *Moral Epistles*, since that is what they are. On this occasion I shall depart from the abstract and tell you, as you desire it, something of the situation in

Rome as it appears to me now. This cannot be repeated but I will do it now at your request. It will not appear among the *Moral Epistles*, in which, indeed, it would have no place.

Some adjustment of taxes has been made in order to lessen the discontent of the Roman plebeians. Caesar had a truly brilliant idea; he thought he would earn immortality by putting an end to all indirect taxation by decree, and for all time. He was dissuaded by various Senators and other experienced men, who showed him how fatal this would be to the state revenue and to the entire establishment. An adjustment was made—and chiefly in the indirect taxes which have caused the trouble, a tax on fried fish and the like, or on purchases above a certain amount—and there is less resentment on that score. The grain supply continues unsatisfactory and Caesar has given awards out of his own fortune to shipowners and middlemen who increase the flow. The frontiers are insecure on the Rhine, Danube and Euphrates, but so they always have been ever since I can remember, and the only real trouble in the Empire comes from Britain, where a bloody rebellion is in progress and has already cost us much ground and many men. If I had had a free hand, when I was able, I might have liked to cut off Britain altogether from the Empire, since I could not see what good it was to Rome, and since it lies behind a most inhospitable stretch of water anyhow. My views, however, could never prevail in such a matter. Romans are superstitiously attached to the ideas of empire, inviolable frontiers, far-off defenses, unable or unwilling to see that if Rome itself fails, these remote protections will avail us nothing. I have been severely criticized for refusing to engage in a war of conquest against Parthia when this seemed feasible a few years ago. I have always been quite content without such adventures, and would rather make peace than war any day.

But let me come to the more succulent dishes for which, I can tell, you have a frustrated appetite. Caesar is obsessed with the idea of marrying Poppaea, who has, with all the arts of her experienced and avid femininity, made herself completely necessary to him. Thus he has sent away Octavia in preparation for a divorce, but, since the discontent of the people in the city grew more obvious every day, he is now, I am told, considering the recall of Octavia. Such chopping and changing will alter nothing and it is my belief that he will eventually marry Poppaea, although I avert my eyes at even the thought of what may happen along the way. He does not give up, even in Poppaea's presence, the throng of concubines and catamites whom he has kept in attendance since he was eighteen years old. None of these has power over him in a civic or political sense, and none, I suspect, has any desire to rule or even to influence his conduct. Some may even love him, as a favorite domestic animal may love even the wickedest master. The slave boy Sporus, whom Caesar married in mockery of all our most ancient religious ceremonies—having castrated him first—is one of these, and so, I am glad to say, is the Asian girl Acté, whom I introduced to Caesar's house more than five years ago in a vain attempt to counteract the imperious fascinations of Poppaea. These are slaves, although now set free, and I have constantly observed that although Caesar spends a great deal of his time with slaves, who often seem to be the only persons with whom he feels free, he is nevertheless influenced by nobility and ancestral renown, for which he has a resentful, angry and dangerous kind of respect. Poppaea dwells upon this, with advantage to herself, since her ancestry is beyond reproach. I think the way in which

Caesar has forced or bribed Roman knights to go on the stage, and Senators to attend his obscene private spectacles, among other things, proves what I say: he instinctively respects, and possibly also fears, the institutions he humiliates. That is why he does it.

I am leaving to the last a piece of news I could be happy not to communicate or even to know. Cornelius Sulla has been murdered. There is no question about the event: it took place several days ago at Marseilles, where he had been for only a week in his new office. I am told the deed was committed by a centurion from Rome, at the head of a mission sent by Tigellinus. What version will be cooked up and served to the Senate and people of Rome I do not yet know: the news itself is horrendous and cannot really be concealed in its true character for long, but a pretense will certainly be made, as always. Perhaps he, too, the least troublesome of men, will be accused of treason and conspiracy. So the noblest blood of Rome is spilled, week after week, in a vain effort to ensure that perfect security which, under our present system of tyranny, can never be attained. Other deeds of the same nature may be expected— Plautus next, perhaps; and as for myself, I have no illusions. I am ready.

Never before have I entrusted so much to writing. I do so because I have faith in your messenger, but also because I am under the strong impression that nothing I say or do makes much difference any more. It is my duty to my wife and family, among whom I include many faithful slaves, to remain among the living if possible, but when that is no longer possible I must go with dignity and decorum. I wish I could see you safely established in a quiet country life before that moment.

The less attention you pay to the affairs of the imperial

court the better off you will be, and I have only mentioned them in response to what seemed an urgent request. Those among whom you live and work should not expect you to be better informed than they are. You can tell them truthfully that our relation is that of a teacher and student in philosophy, and that you are not responsible for anything I have ever said or done in other fields. As between Zeno and Epicurus on that subject, although I do not repudiate anything I have previously written, I must say that now I think Epicurus was right. Meditate upon it, and when you have more time . . .

Lucilius to Seneca (a fragment):

. . . one has just come from Asia who says that Plautus is dead, killed by a centurion from Rome who was in turn under command of Pelago, one of Nero's eunuchs. Perhaps you already know this, but I did not, and since the wayfarer was thrown ashore in Sicily by storm and wind, he may indeed be ahead of the official news. He is in no condition to talk much, and is a prey to numerous fears which cause him to tremble and stammer, but I think he was of the household of that unlucky young prince. From what he says, Rubellius Blandus was naked at midday, preparing for his gymnastic exercises, when the centurion from Rome broke in, with his century at the door, and slew him in the presence of the eunuch. The idea that Plautus might be Nero's successor, if Rome should have the good fortune to survive, has been very widespread and we have heard it often even in Sicily.

I weep for that honest young man who was, on his

mother's side anyhow, of the Julian line, and worthy of his ancestors. But most of all, Seneca, I ask, what next? Is anybody safe? What of you, what of me? If you go, do you think for one moment that I could survive? I do not say this in an ignoble scurry of excitement over my own fate, which I can measure when it comes, but because my soul rebels at the thought of an endless series of such murders and an impoverishment of the Roman Republic at its very source and origin, its men.

Think of your own words on the death of Gaius Caligula: *When the delinquent has an incurable soul he needs to die; sometimes the best work of mercy is to bestow death.* How is the state of things different now, after twenty years? Is it not, rather, worse, if there are gradations of infamy?

Never have the Romans accepted the hereditary principle for the rule of the state. That was monarchy, and we expelled it from our system long ago. The Republic has fallen into the hands of one single family for the past half century, it is true, but almost entirely by military accident. We all know that the Deified Claudius was fleeing from the palace, fearful of sharing the death of his nephew Caligula, when the bloodstained praetorians, unable to think of any alternative, dragged him out from behind the curtains and proclaimed him Emperor. What principle of the Republic was involved? Or what was at stake when Agrippina murdered her husband and made her son Emperor before the people or the Senate had had a chance to draw breath? These successive usurpations and tyrannies have not destroyed the memory of free institutions among Romans. They have merely made it difficult or impossible to refer to our liberties in public. What liberty is this, that must be

) 5 3 (

secret? And what is the use of remembering our institutions when they no longer are allowed to act in the name they bear?

You, Lucius Annaeus Seneca, have taught me well, perhaps too well, and I cannot dispel from my own mind the thought that you may in this extremity come to some decision in the public interest. I know the dangers as well as you do. I do not know the exact details of the circumstances from day to day, as perhaps you do. Even if you stay in the country almost all the time, some of your villas are very near to Rome, almost within the city. There must be hundreds of Romans who feel, as I do, that a word from you would be most valuable in this hour; they must go to you, since you are never far from them. Do they not think, as I do, that the time has come for men of action and men of wisdom to strive, together, to save what can still be saved from the present nightmare?

Forgive my frank and downright language. My messenger is secure and you know me well enough to realize that I never could speak thus if I did not feel that I must. To me it seems that this continuous blood-letting, almost always of the best, the most honest, and when not, of brave men no worse than the rest, must in the end put an end to Rome. Who can want to live in a state of slaves and slaves only? And what else will it be if this terror prevails without interruption or opposition? There are so few left with genuine authority—the authority of Cicero in exile, for example, which has nothing whatsoever to do with the authority of public office—that many minds, not only my own, must turn to you. You alone retain to this day . . .

Seneca to Lucilius (a small part of a long letter):

. . . so there must be no more of this correspondence, by which I mean, on such subjects. If I have any "authority," in the sense you indicate, it must be used to put a stop to such letters. The "authority" of Cicero, by the way, if I may point it out, is felt more strongly by posterity than by his contemporaries, who were much more likely to act, when it came to action, under the authority of Caesar.

My age alone, sixty-eight well past, although not so great as to constitute an obstacle to many men of a different constitution, is too great for me to contemplate any return to worldly affairs. I have lived austerely, in spite of my many houses and the lavish table I have set (of necessity) for others. I do not excuse myself for contradictions; I acknowledge them; I think them inseparable from the nature of mankind. I only pursue wisdom; I have never attained it.

Now, let this not put an end to our correspondence by any means, but let it return to those cooler and higher levels on which it used to dwell. I am no less than human if I love to inculcate those virtuous maxims which I have so often failed to put into practice.

And, to add one more contradiction to the rest, I may descend once more to the level of palace gossip, just for your enlightenment during difficult days: the key to the public troubles is a private one. Nero is himself bloodthirsty and derives some sensuous pleasure, to me unknown, from the act of killing; I have told you so before; he takes pleasure in the death of a harmless cat; and if this is so, how much greater must be the pleasure in a human death? If it is a noble Roman whose house contains many senatorial portraits, would this pleasure not be greatly enhanced? I think so. But what I want to tell you, for your most private information, is that this natural disposition is enormously aggravated by the ministrations of Poppaea, whose soul burns for vengeance upon an almost limitless number of men and women who have shown contempt for her in the past. She is as relentless as she is shameless. Upon her list of victims will be not only her own detractors but her paramours, and not only her paramours but those who have since fallen to the embraces of her paramours. It is as dangerous to be her friend as to be her foe. The power she exercises over Caesar is complex and to many will remain incomprehensible. Although still beautiful beyond almost any comparison in Rome, she is a good deal older than the Emperor and might have been expected to wane upon him with the years. Not so: she is more powerful today than she was five years ago when her husband Otho (who was, as they say, also Nero's) first began to sing her praises to Caesar. I have watched her climb and know how relentless, how utterly controlled and single-minded she is in her purposes. She is not swayed by passion, whim or fear. Unlike most of our noble ladies, she is impervious to the storms she creates. I have never seen her change color or falter in her breath in any circumstance, nor does she betray any feeling at all unless it suits her purposes to do so, and in that case she parades it.

For the ruin of the state we have a very bad ruler, the worst of a long line, but any hope there might have been for his improvement is destroyed by this woman, whose influence at every point is vile and vicious. Their very relationship is vicious in the sense that it is by her wiles, her inventions (her vicious inventions) and by her willingness to share their pleasures that she won and kept his interest. How many noble Roman ladies could be found who would share—well, I shall not elaborate the thought. But Poppaea has added something which has become of supreme concern to Caesar: she has convinced him that she (and she alone) can bear him a child, which, with the life he leads, is an achievement. She has had the aid of certain astrologers in this, but of course she does not spare time or money in her contrivances, and the astrologers are cunning. Caesar wants a child for two reasons, for his own vanity (a continuation of his poetic genius, let us say) and for the line of power. It is obvious that any son he had, at the moment of assuming the virile toga, would become a danger to his own rule and would be put to death as mercilessly as was Britannicus. Caesar does not see so far in advance; at this moment he only wants a son, and he has been superstitiously persuaded that Poppaea alone can give him one. This does not deter him from showing the most puerile jealousy to the son she has with her (Rufinus Crispus, by one of her husbands), who is now fifteen years of age and infuriates the Emperor by playing soldierly games and giving orders to his companions. The boy will be ready for the white toga in another year and I wonder if he will live long enough to assume it. There have been many stepsons in the house of Julius and Claudius—stepsons adopted, as was Nero himself; and Poppaea's boy may not live to see the day. It is a son of his own that Caesar wants.

In the meantime it is said that Poppaea must go away for a while and Octavia must return, in order to calm the generally disorderly instincts of the people in the city. I doubt if this will make any difference. The descent upon which we are far advanced will not change its direction. The evil is too deep.

Now that I have said so much I will repeat that I am too old, tired and unhopeful (in a society of this nature) to make any effort toward the public good. Let us speak of other things. I have failed, yes, but is it not true that Aristotle also failed? He had a different instrument, but it is the effort itself that is doomed to failure. Let you, Lucilius, be the exception! Let us talk of the pleasures of thought, of the pursuit of wisdom, of the tranquillity that comes when . . .

IV

THE LONG, warm October days, moving now into November without perceptible change, brought Octavia into a dreamy state of mind which, without touching on anything so sharp as happiness or soft as content, contained glimpses of both, with the particular solace of being away from Rome added. She had never a day and scarcely even an hour without anxiety in Rome. Here in the Campania, in a country house which had belonged to her mother, she could fill the uneventful season with her own half-childish pleasures, the walk in the woods, the games in the garden with her slave girls no older than herself, the reading and music and the friendly, quiet talk, which, taken all together, soothed and sustained her, more or less unconsciously, in the same way that she was soothed and sustained by the beauty of the autumn leaves or the silence of the sudden twilight. She had no more hope of an issue from her dire situation than ever, and no more desire to find one, but her whole bruised being responded to the grace of repose. It brought with it a mysterious sensation of forgetfulness, deliciously unknown, as if she had acquired the right to expunge from her memory many shadows, and was thus, by all those outside her own walls, no longer remembered. In the unavoidable moments of thought she herself knew that this was illusion; she could neither forget nor be forgotten; but it was the spell of the autumn days to which she yielded with gratitude.

Domitilla and Claudilla, they were called, the two girls who were now constantly with her. These diminutives, suggesting charm and affection as well as youth, were not the result of condescension toward servitude: many highborn Roman matrons had similar names, even long after they had ceased to be suitable. The two girls, born in the imperial household, were sisters or half-sisters and had been brought up with the daughters of Claudius; to Octavia it was not always easy to remember her own power over them, her playmates and friends, or the immensity of her own rank. Indeed the word "empress" sounded alien to her ears, as it did to most Romans, and was in little use: the old formulae of equality between citizens (although not to slaves) had long outlasted the realities of the Republic. She talked to Domitilla and Claudilla more easily than to her own sister Antonia, and was happier with them, if the word could be used of her at all, than with anybody else. Thus the three of them became, in the quiet freedom of Octavia's exile (which looked like a form of imprisonment to others), inseparable once more, as they could not be in Rome, and appeared to be, for long stretches of time, unaware of the clouds that hung over them all alike.

Then there was one other. Eucaerus of Alexandria had received a liberal education in his own language and was especially gifted for music and poetry. He was twenty-four years old, a tall, dark-eyed, serious young man with the long fingers of a lute player, a voice of low and thrilling intensity when he chanted Greek poetry, but gentler, sadder and higher when he sang romances to the lute. The girls could not decide among them as to which was his greater talent, the songs to the lute or those wonderful passages and whole scenes—sometimes by reading and sometimes by memory—from the Athenian tragedies. They could spend hours listening to him, and did.

Only at times Claudilla and Domitilla noticed, as Octavia never did, how mournfully the Greek slave's eyes dwelt on the face of his imperial mistress, and how, in certain very affecting passages in the tragic poets, his voice and eyes alike were filled with tears. Octavia attributed his emotion to the powers of Euripides, perhaps, but the girls noticed that he was most deeply moved in the poetic speeches which bore some relation, near or far, to Octavia's own character and situation. Once, in the *Antigone*, he almost broke down, and had to lower his head and breathe heavily before he could go on. It was possible to understand that his own fate as a slave in a foreign country contributed to his melancholy, but there was some added sorrow, Domitilla and her sister were sure, in these days of late October and early November, something that had not been in his beautiful face when they first beheld it. The condition of an educated or talented Greek slave, highly favored in a

household, was not an immeasurable hardship; it had freedom, almost certainly, and perhaps also fortune as its reward sooner or later; in this case there was a deeper sadness.
Eucaerus had not been long in the house and spoke little,
except in song.

They were thus engaged in the garden when the messengers arrived from Rome—Octavia in a chair, her head in
her hands, the girls on the steps at her feet, their embroi-
dery fallen from idle hands as they listened: Eucaerus was
singing. The master of the household did not even wait for
him to finish the song, but came down the steps straight-
way to Octavia and said the words almost in a whisper,
bowing over her: "Messengers from Rome."

She dropped her hands from her face and turned pale.
One hand went out to Eucaerus to silence him.

"From Caesar?" she asked.

She could tell by his pitying glance, even before he answered her, that this was so. She got to her feet with difficulty.

"I will receive them," she said, and motioned to the three
slaves to stay where they were. She was able to walk in
perfect dignity, although slowly, up the four broad, shal-
low steps to the terrace and then through the doors to the
house. Claudilla, Domitilla and Eucaerus followed her
course with wide, fear-stricken eyes. No good could come
of a message from Caesar. They did not speak to each other
but they came closer together, as if for protection.

After about ten minutes Octavia returned, still walking
very slowly. There was no expression in her face but there
was no color either: the skin was white, white, white.

"Eucaerus," she said in a low voice, "will you sing that
song again? From the beginning, please, and finish it this
time."

He took up his lute and sang the song through to the end. Claudilla and Domitilla thought his voice had never before touched them so deeply. Octavia seemed frozen in her great armchair with her hands to her head. When it was over she thanked the slave and sighed. Her glance swept the autumn leaves at the edge of the park, and the light that was beginning to go from them.

"We are going to Rome tomorrow," she said gently, after a long pause.

The girls bowed their heads; Eucaerus did not stir; he was waiting.

"I do not want to force anybody to go with me," she said.

"We must go with you, Lady," both the girls said, almost in the same moment.

"Yes, perhaps you must," Octavia said, sadly. "We have been together for so long. And—and—well, wherever you are, you are still mine and they would find you. I could set you free, and will do so, but it would make no difference."

"Lady, we cannot leave you."

She sighed again.

"I'm afraid that is true. And you might be safer with me than away from me. I do not know. I know almost nothing now."

Into the silence which followed, and which lasted some time while they all reflected, the voice of the young Greek, trembling with audacity, but low and true in tone, was heard to say: "Lady!"

Octavia turned toward him.

"Eucaerus," she said, "can I help you?"

"Lady, do I go too?"

"Oh, no," she said. "You have never been in my household in Rome. Your place is here, where we found you."

"But this house and everything in it, including its slaves, must be yours, Lady."

"That is so," Octavia said slowly, thinking it over. "There is no reason why I cannot still command what is my own. But . . . but of course . . . They have exact lists of all who came here with me. Since everything I do seems to be wrong, it would probably be wrong of me to add even one person."

"Lady," that same low, scarcely audible voice said, "if I cannot come with you, I shall die here."

There was something in his intensity that alarmed her; her hands fluttered and she rose to go inside the house.

"Poor slave, poor boy," she said in haste, "that may happen anywhere. You are safer here than in Rome."

As she turned toward the steps something happened—some movement occurred and he was there, kneeling at her feet. He had been at the side in the dimming light and now here he was, actually barring her way, and she had not even seen him move. She put her hand to her head, bewildered.

"Take me with you, Lady," he pleaded, "or I die."

"Eucaerus," she said gently.

"One poor lute player, among the hundreds who will be going tomorrow," he said. "One poor Greek slave. They will not notice. There are so many. Lady, I beg for my life."

She turned away from him to go up the steps. Her voice almost failed her.

"If I can," she said, "I will do as you wish."

The girls followed her into the house. They, too, had been startled at the passion in the voice of Eucaerus, but they were not prepared to see their mistress stumble on the steps, or to see the glitter of tears in her eyes.

"Find out," she said to the girls as they crossed the atrium to her own apartments, "find out what he did before we came here. What was his work, I mean. He has been with us these last ten days because you discovered his talents as a singer and lute player, but he must have done some other work before that. If it was very important work I can hardly move him without causing some chatter. I never thought to ask. I suppose he was bought in the market at Naples sometime recently. He was never here before, so far as I remember. I could, of course, ask the master of the household, but he would merely say that everything was mine to command, and I know it isn't."

"Could it be," Claudilla asked fearfully, not raising her eyes, "could it be dangerous to add him to the Rome household just now?"

"Everything I do is dangerous," Octavia said. They were whispering, even in the atrium, because there were spies in every shadow. "His voice—it went through me—I can hardly leave him here after that prayer. I do not know what it is, but I cannot. And then perhaps, if there are really anxious days ahead, I will be grateful for his singing . . . Find out, find out for me! If his work was extremely important, such as keeping the accounts for the whole household, or anything else of that category, it would be difficult to take him away without causing remark."

"I do not think his work was so very important," Domitilla ventured, "because he has not been here long enough to get such work. I have heard that he was brought here no more than a month, at most, before we came, probably less than that. He was only a slave at table when we first noticed him."

Thus it was that Octavia, through sheer compassion for a fellow creature whose fate seemed almost worse than her own, put weapons into the hands of her enemies. For the slave Eucaerus had been assigned to no essential work at the villa and could well be spared, or so they said; and he was included in the great train of persons and chattels which set forth on the following morning, under an especially heavy guard, for the city and the court.

Seneca to Lucilius (an excerpt):

. . . so there is a tremendous agitation of which nobody can foresee the result. The crowds are knocking down and destroying all those statues of Poppaea which were so recently put up in public places, and are restoring the statues of Octavia which they have taken from the Palatine gardens. Mobs roam the streets, cheering for Octavia and the Emperor. They think, poor fools, that because he has bidden her back to Rome he really wants her; they think Poppaea's day is over; they believe all sorts of unwarranted things about Caesar's justice and generosity. They are going at it with such fury that if Poppaea were to appear in public (of which there is no chance at all) they would probably tear her to shreds. In this way they can only enrage the prince. I know him well. He will not forgive this outburst, nor indeed, I think, the poor lady who is its innocent cause. It is the worst thing that could have happened to her at the moment. I stay away, of course—I could never venture into Rome unbidden, at this time—but I cannot prevent a stream of visitors who come here at all hours of the day and night to tell me what is going on. I warn you to say nothing and do nothing that might indicate special knowledge of these events. Better, by far, to seem ignorant; let those who surround you know more than you do at all times. For spies and informers are every-where, and my judgment is that the Emperor is in a greater state of susceptibility to them, and of ferocity toward their victims, than ever before. The way of Poppaea's ambition will be bloodstained indeed, for Caesar cannot endure to be thwarted; he has had his first experience of the willfulness of that Roman mob which has always been his willing play-thing hitherto, and it will cut deep in his nature. Nobody is safe now, and you, as a known pupil of mine, will be under special suspicion. I cannot pledge myself to write to you again soon, for your sake as much as my own (and more). When a more peaceful season is upon us . . .

Lucilius to Seneca (part of a long letter):

. . . because you know the slave and are aware that he is trustworthy. Otherwise I should be silent at this time. But I must tell you that the news of Octavia's return to Rome has produced almost the same effect in Sicily as elsewhere. There have been prolonged demonstrations, in some of which the public officials took part. Her statues are vener-ated and surrounded by offerings. There has been a cloud of information, true or false, and many indiscretions on the part of persons in high places. On your warning I have been remote from it all, said nothing, done nothing, and if any spy or informer reports otherwise, it is the basest of lies, pure and malevolent invention. I would not imperil your life or the fortunes of your family, aside from my own interests, by any rash word or deed at such a time. For if I should fall now, as so many others have, there would be quite certainly an attempt to make you responsible for my supposed crimes. And if, as I must guess, there are now to be many more trials and executions, it is part of my duty to remain alive and untouched if any such result can be honorably attained. You will readily see how, even here in Sicily, our fates, yours and mine, are thought to be entangled, and hardly a day passes when some officer of the state does not ask me how or where you are or what you are thinking. I will be careful, if there is the possibility of . . .

Seneca to Lucilius (marked "in haste") :

There must be no more correspondence between us at present. I am sending this by your same faithful slave because I have learned his worth, but I do not believe any further word between us would be wise until matters have cleared, at least a little, so that one might be confident of perhaps a week's repose. I cannot bar my doors to everybody who comes, and I greatly fear that some who have come in the past few days, although honorable citizens, are not likely to retain their freedom for long. Proposals have been made to me which I refuse to write down in plain language. It is senseless for any Roman, however noble and devoted to his country, to think of me, at my age, as a possibility for power. I have had power and I regret it. Nor will I take part in any schemes, any plots or plans. Yet those who do (and who will not be deterred by me) insist upon thrusting me into the middle of their vain dreams. Thus, as you see, my situation is suddenly more dangerous, more immediately dangerous, than it has been since Caesar said farewell. For myself, I am ready; I have always told you so, and you cannot doubt me; but it is a clear duty to my wife and family to avoid the catastrophe as long as possible. This may not be long. For your own sake, just so, desist from any communication with me until I have told you that we may resume, as of old, a flow of thought in philosophy itself, unfettered by the dire happenings of our degenerate time. I may never be able to say this. If so, I trust you to remember my lesson rather than my life, since the first was pure. And you, until ambition caused you to seek the public service (in which, I admit, I found you a place as high as your merit and age would countenance), you were my most promising pupil. I will not dwell upon it. Farewell.

In Poppaea's apartments on the Palatine, secluded now and under strong guard, Sophronius Tigellinus was welcome. He was, indeed, responsible for her safety, and had himself chosen from the praetorian cohorts those most trusted detachments which could best ensure it. He was often there, and had, almost alone, to endure the extremities of her icy rage and scorn. Caesar, a prey to many disagreeable emotions and sensations during those days, feared Poppaea's anger so much that he made his visits rare; they would have been rarer still if he had dared to make them so. She could not go out of her apartments, where, with all the space and splendor, she had nobody but her slave women for companions, and they lived in such terror of her that they were almost beyond communication. Her son Rufinus could come and go, a mystified boy of fifteen, but she dared not have him much in the house for fear that Caesar, who had taken a strong dislike to him, might come in and find him there. Thus it was Tigellinus who became almost her only link with a world she had so lately ruled as her own.

She did not accept and never could accept a situation of the kind. She knew it was only temporary; Caesar had told her so often, and she knew him well enough to realize that he had innumerable reasons for speaking the truth in this matter; but the humiliation, however temporary, was the severest her proud temper had ever endured. It was intolerable to think that the Roman mob, for which she had nothing but contempt, could impose its own will in anything that concerned her; and it was equally intolerable to think that the colorless, empty girl Octavia, who had never even been to bed with the Emperor and was, according to the best reports of the best informers, a virgin, should have the semi-divine honors as Caesar's wife. She, Poppaea, was Caesar's true wife, as she had been for five years, and would be so recognized by the whole world—under the name of empress, what is more, a word she relished—as soon as she could overcome the opposition of the circumstances. Thus she had a strong natural sympathy for Tigellinus, whose aims were the same as hers, and whose advance to high position she had greatly aided. They were fellow conspirators in essence because they were agreed to work together in dominion over Caesar's mind and power, which they were well qualified—almost alone qualified—to do at this moment in time. There had been others before them, but at this moment they had no rivals for his attention in the matters they both had at heart.

Even so, Poppaea was not indulgent to Tigellinus. He felt the weight of her anger whenever he came to her presence. She thought he should have been able, by his central position and his familiarity with Caesar, to prevent the return of Octavia and the outburst of Roman popular feeling. She considered it his duty to her, Poppaea, as the author of his greatness, to do her will. He was prepared to do so but had to impose obstacles to her headlong flight: it was like trying to dam an irresistible stream.

"Where is the old fool, Seneca?" she asked, looking upon him as from a great height. They were in formal gilded armchairs a few feet apart, with an Asian rug between them. He was uncomfortable and looked it.

"He was at his villa Nomentana until yesterday," Tigellinus said. "Now he has moved off into the hills. He has had some dubious visitors."

"He is himself dubious, and in fact more than dubious," Poppaea said. "I have no doubt that he is a traitor. When will you find the evidence so that we may get rid of him for good and all?"

"It will come, Lady," Tigellinus said, as submissively as any slave. His flashing armor and golden insignia did not obscure his subservience to her. "We are collecting the facts."

"If you do not have the facts you can make them for yourself," Poppaea said coldly. "When have you become so scrupulous about facts? I can mention a number of cases in which you had no facts at all, but obtained the heads of the denominated subjects—and their estates as well—without any trouble. You will never deceive me by your reverence for facts, Tigellinus. And if you think I forget anything, you are mistaken. I am familiar with every step in your rise. I arranged most of them."

"Yes, Lady."

"And the girl Octavia, too, What have you done? What will you do? She must be, and let us be plain, she must be destroyed. Completely. Otherwise there is no assurance that she will not come up again, as she has done just now, to ruin every reasoned or reasonable arrangement it is possible to make. I am a prisoner here. What are you doing?"

"I have some new evidence which I may be able to put before Caesar. He is ready for it, I assure you. He asks nothing better. But it is in his nature to let the popular excitement die down before he does anything in the opposing sense. I want to speak at the right time."

"Now is the right time," she said composedly. "If you are afraid, I am not. But what evidence can you have which would shake Octavia's position? We have already accused her of being barren, which was rather bold in view of the fact that she has had no opportunity to be anything else. We sent her away from Rome on that ground. It is a point difficult to prove, under these circumstances."

"This is a quite different point," Tigellinus said. "It is adultery."

"No!" said Poppaea, admiringly. "How could you make that line of attack? The whole world knows that she has never looked at a man. Nor, to my knowledge, has any man ever looked at her. How can that frigid skeleton be accused of anything so unlikely?"

"There are possibilities," Tigellinus said judiciously.

"Name them," Poppaea commanded. "And I warn you that even Caesar will be slow to believe."

"She has a favorite slave," Tigellinus said slowly. "His name is Eucaerus. He is a Greek from Alexandria. He sings to the lute and he also chants scenes from the tragedies. Octavia found him at her villa in the Campania when she was there just now. She has brought him back to Rome with her. He still sings to her every day."

Poppaea leaned forward. The jewels on her bosom moved and glittered with her breathing, but none of her many jewels were more brilliant than her dark eyes.

"Adultery?" she said, on a rising inflection.

"Perhaps," Tigellinus said coolly, meeting her eyes with

a courageous stare. "Who can tell? These are secrets. But what is to prevent the charge being made? The only possible witnesses could be slaves. Slaves will say anything under torture. The case is not difficult to present."

"It is no proof," she said, sitting back again, but with an air of triumph. "It is no proof at all, Tigellinus, and you know it. But it might very well be proof enough for Caesar. He does not want much. He is ready for any pretext to get rid of her. His patience is now exhausted, as it should be after the disturbances of this past week. If the charges were made—if, for instance, I should make the charge myself, in private conversation—would you be ready to bring forth some kind of evidence, enough to justify the examinations under torture? Enough to give Caesar an excuse or a pretext or an appearance of justification? No more is needed. He wants to be bold but he needs a reason. Will you give him one?"

"I will find something," he said slowly. They exchanged a long look. "I want a little time."

"Not much," she said decisively. "There is every need of haste. You cannot require more than a few hours, a day at most, to put together what Caesar will ask of you. Enough, that is, to make the charge. I will make the charge myself, privately, and as soon as possible. He will then ask you what you know of it. Then is when you must be strong."

"I will do it," he said.

"You will have no cause to regret what you do," she said nobly. "It is a service to the state."

He gave her a rather meaning look, at which she averted her glance for a moment. Even to Poppaea the idea of explicit connivance with this man was unwelcome; it irked that pride which, however maltreated by herself and others, was the most powerful of her native emotions, alike for strength and for weakness. She could never altogether forget the array of senatorial portraits in her grandfather's house.

"Go now," she said, "and take with you the boy Rufinus. He is in the next room I think. Take him to the garden or to the guardhouse or where you like. Caesar is coming."

And indeed, as Tigellinus took his leave, one of Poppaea's women appeared in the doorway to make the conventional sign (a variation on the Roman salute) that the Emperor was near. Poppaea rose with her unfailing grace and approached the door, her eyes and her hands, the very posture of her sumptuous body, conveying love's eager expectancy. Nero was in the doorway.

"Hail, Caesar," she said.

AT CAIUS CALPURNIUS PISO's villa on the Appian Way, some two hours from Rome, a fateful talk was taking place at this very time. Two Roman knights, friends of the noble Piso, had come to see him by arrangement, and in view of the nature of their business they had repaired to the big apple orchard on a hill behind the house, where no slaves or women might overhear what was said. One of them was tribune of a praetorian cohort and the other a centurion. The tribune, Subrius Flavus, had for years enjoyed the friendship of Faenius Rufus, co-commander (with Tigellinus) of the praetorian cohorts, and bore a high reputation in the city as well as in his privileged and chosen band of guardsmen. The centurion was Sulpicius Asper, a handsome, hot-blooded young man with distinguished relatives and a wide popularity in the legions where he had served. Neither of them was conspicuous enough in the life of the capital to have been followed on this journey to Piso's country house, but they had, even so, taken the precaution to start in another direction and then to divert their course when they were well out of the city. Neither had ever come under suspicion of political activity or, indeed, of anything else which could be regarded as forbidden by present law or custom, indulgent as both had become. Piso knew them separately and together, as banqueting companions and familiars of the palace, and was quite ready to trust them even after they had made it clear that theirs was no common errand.

"I agree with everything you say," Caius Piso told them, pausing under an apple tree to look at the setting sun. "You cannot feel more strongly than I do about the criminal madness of Caesar and his favorites. This is the worst of all: even Caligula could not compare with this. But in common sense I am compelled to ask what chance, what possible chance, have any of us, together or separately, against imperial power? *How* can we act? You imply that there is something in particular that I can do but I cannot discern what it may be. The Senate is helpless, as you have seen. How can a few individual citizens do what the Senate itself cannot do?"

The tribune Subrius, as the elder of the two knights, answered for both.

"It all hangs upon the single life of Caesar himself," he said. "Once that is gone, there is no successor. He has murdered them all. The praetorians and the legions will choose his successor. It should be a man of the noblest ancestry, one whose forefathers built the Republic, one who believes in our freedoms and has the respect of the people. Such a man, in fact, as you."

There was a long silence while the two knights studied Piso's unyielding frown and firmly set lips. Finally Piso spoke, slowly and as if painfully, with that accent of sincerity which had been his chief asset as orator in public.

"I have never thought of such a thing for myself," he said, "and I do not intend to think of it now. It is true that Caesar's power expires with his life. I suppose you have thought of what that means. You have evidently thought of what comes afterward. Have you truly considered what comes before—that is, the means by which Caesar's life will be ended?"

"We have," they both said at once, and then Subrius took it up.

"We have thought of every detail," he said eagerly, "and we are ourselves willing to be the instruments. It should be in public and possibly at an entertainment, where the opportunities are greater—the theater, or the gladiators' games. But I want to tell you two things, Piso. The hour of confusion after Caesar's life has ended is important because in that hour the future will be decided and we must be ready. The other thing is that you have referred to us as 'a few individuals.' We are, as I tried to say earlier, already numerous. We have every advantage with the troops. The number of nobles and knights who have shown a desire to work with us would surprise you. We did not want to come to you until things had developed toward some sort of comprehensible plan. But we are not few. We are many."

Caius Piso leaned against an apple tree and sighed. There was another long silence.

"You," he said, looking at Subrius, "are the friend of Faenius Rufus. He is your commanding officer. You know that his associate, Tigellinus, is completely Caesar's slave, or Poppaea's, which comes to the same. His crimes equal theirs and he could never survive them. He is astute. His hatred of Faenius Rufus is obvious. The question then is: where does Faenius Rufus stand? Without him, and without at least some part of the praetorian cohorts, the whole scheme would be quite insane."

"But he is with us!" Subrius protested. "Without him we should be destroyed at once. But the praetorians are more loyal to him than to this upstart Tigellinus, and he can command in a crisis as Tigellinus never could."

"I should like to see some evidence that Faenius Rufus is 'with us,' as you call it," Piso said slowly, looking from one to the other. "It would seem to me to be the principal consideration, so far as the first step is concerned."

"But you can have the evidence whenever you wish!" the younger knight, Sulpicius Asper, intervened eagerly. "He was quite willing to come here today!"

"It is true that he wanted to come," Subrius assented. "I thought his coming here might attract attention, as ours would not. He saw my point. But you know that the insolence of Tigellinus, and the necessity of sharing the command of the guard with him, have eaten into Rufus until he is almost a different man today. His natural openness and frankness and generosity, all those qualities which have made him so popular and respected, are turning sour. He has not been the same since the murder of Agrippina. It was then that he knew there was no end to this tyranny except through death."

"He has also learned, as you may have heard earlier, that he is openly accused of having been one of Agrippina's paramours," Sulpicius put in. "It is not true and it angers him because it is an invention of Tigellinus. The purpose is clear. Like everything else from that source, it is intended to ruin him with Caesar."

"Rufus is a fearless man of high honor," Piso said, meditatively. "If he were with you, it might indeed be possible to carry out your plan."

"You can talk with him when you wish," Subrius asserted. "You will see that I have not misrepresented him."

"We must arrange it then," said Caius Piso with deliberation. He still seemed to be thinking aloud, step by step, as if he had not altogether realized the magnitude of the undertaking put before him. "It should be done without arousing any particular notice. And, of course, I have not yet consented to take part in your plans. I must know a great deal more. I may agree with your feeling and your desire to do something. I must also know whether it presents any possibility of success. I should like to talk to Faenius Rufus, yes. May I leave it to you to arrange this, and soon?"

On their eager consent he went on talking, more or less to himself, although his words were addressed to them.

"But who are the others?" he asked, as if he expected the wind to answer. "You say you are not few but many. I have heard no names mentioned. It would require a considerable number of men in vital positions to bring about such a revolutionary change as you have in mind. I am not afraid of violence. It is worse than useless, however, if it does not attain its object, and if it merely adds more bloodshed to the blood that already disgraces Rome . . . Nor do I see, precisely, what there is for me to do, if you have already planned the crucial deed."

"We are determined," Subrius answered him. "I will give you names well known to you. But we have lacked an imposing leader, one who means something to the people. Yours is the Calpurnian house, just as noble and just as ancient as the Julian or the Claudian, and probably more so. We have chosen you as the man we need for what you call the second step—the creation of a government to succeed this tyranny."

"I don't feel sure of my own significance to the people," Piso said abruptly. "Not at all. Have you talked to Seneca?"

"We have tried on several occasions and with several emissaries," Subrius told him. "The old man will not talk. He says he is too old to think of taking part in any plans. We have been a little afraid of telling him too much—indeed, of telling him the main facts. We have only sounded him out, but of course he can easily guess the part we do not mention. He is extremely astute. He stopped me from speaking, at one moment when I was with him, and said he preferred not to hear any more."

"They say," said the young Sulpicius, "that he now wishes he had never had anything to do with the business of the state. If so"—and his voice grew impatient—"what could he do in his old age?"

"Nobody else has such eminence or such weight," Piso reminded them. "Through all this miserable time, for almost a decade, he has been respected. He has never been blamed for the crimes of his pupil. It would be an advantage—the greatest possible advantage—to have his good will and, if possible, his advice."

"His advice would be to do nothing," the young knight said. "That is, if he were willing to give advice. And anyhow he is surrounded by spies and informers. We believe they have tried to poison him in just these recent weeks. Since he eats nothing but berries and fresh fruit and nuts— well, it's hard to poison that provender."

Piso smiled: the young man did not greatly value the old one.

"I wonder if you might have better luck with him than I did, or than anybody else who has tried," Subrius Flavus put in. "We all know the weight of his name, his reputation. Perhaps he would listen to you. But it would have to be done with the utmost caution."

"His nephew Lucanus has no love for Caesar," Piso remarked. "The rivalries of poets are bitter." He referred to the known fact that Caesar had caused Lucan's poetry to be suppressed. "He was once a friend of mine."

"Then," Subrius said eagerly, "see what you can do with Lucanus. During this time you require to decide your own part, you could speak with him and with others. I can give you the list of those who have sworn to be with us when the time comes. Lucan can tell you more about his uncle than anybody. He might be the one who could best speak to the old man. But above all things we want to move soon. There will be few of us left if we do not take action as soon as possible."

"I see that. I do see that. Every day, every day . . . Well, I must still think. You will give me that list of which you spoke . . . I may go into Rome tomorrow and will try to have a word with one or two friends. Perhaps I can talk to Lucan. I will try not to delay you. But it is not a thing to which I, or anybody else, could give an immediate answer. There is too much in it. May we meet again in, say, two days' time?"

It was left thus: that Piso would make his cautious inquiries and talk to them further. He could feel their impatience tugging away at their good manners: they wanted a quick answer and immediate action. For him, with vast estates and a network of family connections, it was not so easy, although his heart responded to their desire for the decisive blow; his risks were so much greater than theirs. He could not see, furthermore, what his contribution was to be in the immense changes that were to come if they had their way. Did they actually think of him as a possible Caesar? He had never had such dreams. It did not seem to him an idea that could be received, even inside his own head, without consternation, and above all he was unwilling to discuss it with anybody else. He could speak of the earlier part of the plan—what he called "the first step"— although it did not sound as if they needed or wanted his participation in it. He could speak of the plan as a whole, with its great glittering promise of a better government for the Republic and the people. Then, gradually, as he grew more familiar with the project, he might derive from the words of trusted men, old friends and others involved, some clear idea of what was expected from him, what he might do to bring about a better state of things.

Piso was not a conspirator by nature; he was not ambitious; he was not secretive; he was not bloodthirsty. He had always had an abundance of everything he needed or wanted. And even so, the two Roman knights had hardly been gone from his house for half an hour before the subtle wine of suggestion began to work on him. He began to think: Well, why not? If it is for me to do it, I must do it. To restore the liberties of the state—what better aim could there be? If it involved the assumption of high office, even the very highest, it might be the only way to make his contribution. His ancestral rank, reaching deep into the origins of the Empire, would justify such an issue. It was new and strange but it was not impossible.

By the time he set forth toward Rome on the following morning, after a restless night, the process of his intellectual conversion was already well advanced. He had not, even to himself, decided anything irrevocable, but he was already finding it fairly natural to think in terms which, twenty-four hours before, would have been utterly alien.

And within a few days the plan of the tribune Subrius, which had sounded altogether new as it was described in Piso's orchard, had involved a wider circle. It seemed that each new recruit to the scheme was eager to bring in others, so that the number of persons actually aware of the conspiracy—not all of them entrusted with its details—grew constantly larger. The intoxication of doing something, at last, or of planning something to be done, was responsible for an enthusiasm among the conspirators which outran all discretion. It was in this rush of hope and confidence that Annaeus Lucanus, the poet Lucan, went out to see his uncle Seneca at his villa Nomentana, the one closest to Rome.

Lucan was bright-eyed, malicious, and as unlike his uncle as could well be imagined, but the attachment of Seneca for the whole family covered all their differences. Even so, it was with an emotion not unlike despair that Seneca heard what his nephew had to say.

"I had some inkling, some hint, some thought of what might be going on," the old man said. They sat in the garden over a cup of wine. "But from what you say I gather that you are yourself involved. That means, I suppose, every member of your family and mine. It is no use for me to protest innocence. Nobody will believe it."

He mused for a while, confronting in all its complexity the future presented by his nephew's words.

"You believe in the success of this mad scheme," he said finally. "You really do not know—I doubt if you can even guess—the extent of the imperial power. It is not only visible. The invisible power is worse, wider and deeper. There are spies everywhere, in every man's household. There is no member of your own family who may not—*may* not—inform against you. There is no slave, however faithful, who can be counted upon any more. Everybody in Rome has learned that the way to wealth and favor is to report the misdoings, true or false, of others. I have had, unfortunately, too many reasons to appreciate the depth and strength of this invisible power. I have known it at close quarters. It was perhaps Tiberius who began it; I think this may be the truth; but it has grown since until it is the central power of the state. There was nothing I could do to destroy it, although I tried at times to soften its tyranny. Along with this, the secret power, there has been a steady breakdown, on the other side, of the law courts which might have opposed it. As we stand today, the Emperor himself—in his own court—is the final judge and in fact the only judge of treason. What chance have you or any of you or all of you against such a system?"

"We begin, remember," said Lucan, somewhat shaken by the old man's vehemence, "by the death of Caesar. Once that has taken place the entire secret system is at a loss. It is no good without a master."

"It is in the hands of desperate men who will do anything to keep their own control," Seneca told him. "It is in the hands of Tigellinus, most of all, at this moment. Do you think there is any mercy or justice in Tigellinus? You might as well expect it of Poppaea. If you proceed with your plans, and they are discovered, as I think they must be, not only the persons actually involved will suffer but every member of their families and almost countless innocent persons who are only suspected of complicity. That is what happens when the rule of law breaks down and one evil man is the whole center of authority in the state."

"We are committed, Uncle," said Lucan. "We can none of us draw back now. We will carry through the entire plan. And not one of us has ever thought of you as a participant in the actual violence of the day Caesar dies. No, indeed. We have some respect for age, for your eminence in wisdom and philosophical statecraft, for—for—well, for you as a Roman. But we should like to think that when that day is over and we must make the Roman Republic live again, we can call upon you for help. We want the mantle of your authority. We want the wisdom of your voice. No other can reassure the people. We can rebuild in your name."

Seneca took a long, cold look at the younger man. His own gaunt face, now so lined by dietary austerities, was gray, worn, sad: he had seen too much of vain hope, and this poet suddenly seemed very far away from him.

"Is it possible," he asked, "that you think of wars and revolutions carried out with my name on your banner? Do you think of me, less than half here, as a leader in a time of trouble? Or is it possible that you, like some other madmen who have come to see me in recent months, actually think of me as a possible Caesar? If so, you are beyond reason or common sense. The most I could ever do, if your plans ever reached the stage of reality, would be to give you some advice. It would not be much but I think it might be good. That is in fact the utmost it would be possible to ask of me at my age and in my condition. Some men at my age—the Divine Augustus, for instance—were well able to command and rule. Not I. I never have been, in truth, and it is much too late to try now. I love and respect a good many of the persons you have named to me as being part of your very daring scheme. I wish you would tell them all that they have no idea, can have no idea, of the depth and width of the secret power, the secret services of betrayal and death, which Caesar owns. Nobody can be trusted any more. And yet, from what you tell me, a very large number of you, knights and nobles of Rome, have trusted not only each other but the slaves and retainers who are always with you. How can you do this? It is insanity for yourselves and destruction for your families. Somewhere, somehow, there will come a betrayal. It is bound to come. The rewards of treachery are too great. Believe me. Forgive, but believe."

Lucan believed, above all, that his uncle was too old and exhausted for any enterprise of high endeavor, but that his mind and heart concurred in approval. He did not understand the warning Seneca gave him: he had, as the old man said, no real acquaintance with the extent of the secret powers, and therefore could scarcely take in even the mention of their existence. It would not have been possible for any man of intelligence to misconceive more completely than Lucan did, the meaning of Seneca's message. As the poet transmitted it to a chosen number of friends, all deep in the conspiracy, the effect of it was simply this: "The old man is with us but can do nothing and will do nothing—too old, weak, worn out with anxiety and no food. But he's with us, he is really with us in spirit. When the time comes we will have his authority behind us, I am sure."

It was in these terms, somewhat more lengthily and with

much explanation, that he gave the news to the woman Epicharis.

Epicharis was one to whom Annaeus Lucanus often had resort in times of anxiety. Her house, although far from mean, was small enough and quiet enough to soothe his jangled nerves after excesses either of pleasure or pain; her arms and voice were soft and her spirit pliant. Whatever his mood, she suited it, and if it were said that she could do the same for others, he had no objection. An exclusive attachment was not to be expected in Rome, unless, indeed, it were for somebody too powerful to tolerate anything else. Lucan was grateful for the hours he could spend with Epicharis and put no guard on his tongue when he talked with her, since she had nothing to do with public matters. It was a surprise, therefore, to hear her flare up at him on this occasion.

"Well, then, what are you waiting for?" she asked. "You talk and talk and talk. Why do you not take a sword and kill the monster? You and all your friends—I am one of you, anyhow by intention—are sworn to kill Caesar and save Rome from further ruin. But why don't you do it? There is no end to his crimes. There will be nothing left if you do not act soon. What is the use of all this waiting and taking counsel and scratching chins? It only puts off the act."

Lucan, astonished, sat up in bed.

"It will come," he said. "But you, my sweet, sound as if you wanted to strike the blow yourself. I did not know you were so filled with the noble passion."

"I may be only a woman," she said, "but I am a Roman, too. My blood boils to see this horrible tyrant go unpunished. There are so many of you, all brave knights and nobles, and how can you wait, how can you hesitate?"

So she spoke, inciting him, and as he was not slow to perceive, she was so sincere that in all probability she spoke in the same way to others whom she knew to be acquainted with the plan. He was troubled to see a woman, even Epicharis—who was so discreet and quiet as to be almost anonymous—thus deep in the secret, and yet he realized that it was not from himself alone, in his scattered but inconsecutive confidences, that she had acquired her knowledge. There must have been a dozen bits of information which, pieced together by her quick and well-centered mind, gave her a very tolerable notion of the entire conspiracy. She was not distracted by court gossip or the talk of the market place; she went out very little; she had few women friends; it was in her own house that she had come by this awareness. He tried to reason with her, to show how difficult it was to choose a place and time for an act which, if it failed, would be fatal to many. It had to succeed: that was its only possible justification. He told her how carefully every possible course had been, and was still being, considered.

"Oh, it is not so difficult," she said, still afire with her impatience. "Caesar loves the water, the boats, the seaside. Get him to Piso's big villa down there at Baiae. It will be easy. He would go for the day, or for a shorter visit, or for the banquet at night."

"We have thought of all that, believe me," Lucan told her, getting into his clothing. "There is one enormous obstacle. One which makes it impossible. Piso refuses."

"Why? How can he? Is he not the heart and center of the whole undertaking? Is *he* afraid?"

"No, it's not that. He is afraid of nothing. But such a deed in his own house—he refuses. It would be sacrilege, and his household gods would be avenged, or so he thinks. I do not know what is so sacred about a house or a table, but these great aristocrats have some exaggerated concepts in that respect. We have already had it out—he will not do it."

"Nero was never held back by household gods," the woman sneered. "He poisoned his brother Britannicus at his own table. How many others, as well? I do not think much of your Piso if he refuses to take such an obvious advantage."

"He is a man of another age, in some respects," Lucan told her. "He thinks of such things, and of family honor, and of ancestors, a good deal more than others do—others, that is, who have just as many reasons for respecting the old beliefs as he has. It is not a discouraging characteristic. If he were in power it would be a guaranty of virtue, at least within limits."

Both were now fully dressed and moved with joined hands into another room.

"I am burning with the desire to do something myself," she said. "It seems to me that the seaside, Baiae or Misenum or Antium, would be the place for such a deliverance. I cannot understand Piso. Even so, since we know that Caesar loves those places and is less on his guard there, the advantages are obvious. I know officers of the fleet who might well be useful. If there were some prepared to stand guard while others—while some of you—did the deed, that would be a very favorable circumstance, wouldn't it?"

He stared at her with gathering horror.

"Do not, dear Epicharis," he said finally, after he had at last realized the depth of her intent," do not do anything, anything at all, I beg of you. I implore you. You could risk all the lives that are involved in the matter—and nothing should be undertaken, anyhow, without the authority of the chief men, the commanders. Don't you understand? It would be dangerous—I cannot tell you how dangerous—to talk to your friends in the fleet, no matter how well you know them. Do nothing, nothing, nothing, I tell you. If there is anything for you to do I will give you the signal when I am authorized to do so. But now, promise me—promise me—you will do nothing."

"You are like all the rest," she said sullenly. "You think a woman is an instrument of pleasure, not fit for anything else, incapable of understanding the high thoughts and deeds of a Roman. You have no idea how I burn with the desire to help save my own country from ruin, and yet I am treated as if I could not even discuss a way out. Very well. Very well. But women have served the state before now."

"Of course, of course," Lucan agreed in haste, anxious above all things to be off now that she had so alarmed him. "Women will have a true part in everything we undertake, believe me. There will be work for you, Epicharis. But not now. Now is the moment for the most extreme secrecy. You must not discuss these matters—they are too dangerous—and you must above all not speak of them to your friends in the fleet. I have confidence in you. Dear Epicharis."

After he had gone he was overcome with doubt and misgiving, above all for his own part in the matter. No woman should be aware of these plans in their present state of flux. Lucan was profoundly aware of his own rashness in speaking to her of his visit to Seneca, but he was also quite certain, from her knowledgeable expressions and lack of all surprise, that the general idea was by no means unknown to her. She had been apprised of it by somebody, and since by now the number of conspirators had so much increased, he

VI

TIGELLINUS, FROWNING at the elaborate tiles of the floor, was justifying himself to Poppaea.

"I cannot arouse Caesar's jealousy on this subject," he said flatly, "precisely because of his indifference to the lady. If he cared anything about Octavia he would, of course, be wild with rage at the thought of any dalliance on her part. As it is, he simply does not care. She can come or go as circumstances make it advisable. She is nothing to him. I have hinted as strongly as possible—I have in fact said flatly—that she is intimate with the Alexandrian slave. It makes no real impression on Caesar. He does not want to see her and in fact does not want to hear about her. He recalled her to Rome as a purely political move, because she is popular with the Romans. That is all."

"I have also asked him," Poppaea said bitterly, "if he wants to be presented with the child of a slave as his heir. Even that does not stir him. Perhaps it is because he has himself frequented so many slaves. He has no shame in it."

"That is not the point," Tigellinus insisted. "If it were you—if any allegation, even the hint of one, should be made about you—it would madden him. It is merely Octavia. She is his unwanted and displeasing sister or step-sister, and he cannot think of her otherwise."

"The pale-faced slut," Poppaea fretted. "The empty, stupid, dying skeleton—that such—!"

After an effort she controlled her anger, as usual, and went on.

"That such a wretched, half-born girl should stand in my way is hard to bear. But there is nothing I have not said to Caesar, and without result. I have repeatedly told him what he must expect from the daughter of Messalina but that does not revolt him. He is without shame for others as for himself. There is some other way, if I could hit upon it."

Tigellinus was reflecting with her.

"It would be best if it were possible to *show* him something," he said slowly. "That might have an effect far beyond mere words. But there is a serious obstacle: that is, what have we to show? I do not believe the girl has committed or is committing any fault."

"If she has not, she will do so in time," Poppaea said imperiously. "She is her mother's daughter. It will come out."

"True of all," she told him, "either I myself or some one
of any women who really knows music and poetry must
hear this sing. It would be best to hear him when he does
not know that any care, except those of Octavia, are floating-
ing. And if, or we, judge that he is really good in the art,
good enough to arouse Caesar's rage, then we must arrange
for the Emperor himself to hear the same thing. It should
be more or less the same thing we have heard, otherwise it
might be different and the results might not be satisfactory".

Timellinus took this in without trouble; he was quick-
witted enough when it came to complexity, even though
Caesar's passion for singing was beyond him.

"I know how to arrange it," he said. "You and one of
your women could be quite safe behind a wall of that small
garden where Octavia sits in the late afternoon. The guards
will take care of you. I know exactly the place. And if it is
your wish, we can put the Emperor there on the next day,
or on the nearest day we can find."

"Good Timellinus," she said. "There is some promise of
success in this. It all depends on whether the boy Sporsing,
therefore, can really sing or not. If it is good he will throw
Caesar into a frenzy, and the frenzy will be against Octavia, of course, not against the boy. Do you see? It will
arouse him to Caesar, as singer and lute player—and he
thinks himself the greatest the world has known—that Octavia is preferring this slave to him. If it is worse than my
estimate it could be anomalous. It could be a serious
offence."

"We shall make it so," Timellinus said, ready to take his
leave. "I think you are mistaken, Lady, in certain matters,
since even Poppaea, that child of all charm—"

"First of all," she told him, "either I myself or some one of my women who really knows music and poetry must hear this slave. It would be best to hear him when he does not know that any ears, except those of Octavia, are listening. And if I, or we, judge that he is really good in his art, good enough to arouse Caesar's rage, then we must arrange for the Emperor himself to hear the same thing. It should be more or less the same thing we have heard; otherwise it might be different and the results might not be satisfactory."

Tigellinus took this in without trouble; he was quick-witted enough when it came to conspiracy, even though Caesar's passion for singing was beyond him.

"I know how to arrange it," he said. "You and one of your women could be quite safe behind a wall of that small garden where Octavia sits in the late afternoon. The guards will take care of you. I know exactly the place. And if it is your wish, we can put the Emperor there on the next day, or on the nearest day we can find."

"Good Tigellinus," she said. "There is some promise of success in this. It all depends on whether the boy Eucaerus, the slave, can really sing or not. If he is good he will throw Caesar into a frenzy, and the frenzy will be against Octavia, of course, not against the boy. Do you see? It will somehow seem to Caesar, as singer and lute player—and he thinks himself the greatest the world has known—that Octavia is preferring this slave to him. It is far worse than any adultery could be nowadays. It could be a crowning offense."

"We shall make it so," Tigellinus said, rising to take his leave. "I admire your intellect, Lady, as extravagantly as I admire your beauty. You think of all things."

And he made it his business to investigate immediately around Octavia's villa for the means of bringing concealed listeners within earshot of the small garden. Since the praetorian guard had full control of the Palatine Hill it was not difficult. Tigellinus himself commanded the cohorts which immediately protected Caesar's palace and, across park and garden, the villa pavilion which had now been assigned to Octavia, as well as the larger villa on the palace side of the garden which was occupied by Poppaea. To get these central functions under his exclusive command had cost Tigellinus a year of effort and all the favoritism which he could call upon Caesar to bestow; normally Rufus, by seniority and public standing, would have retained the charge; but now that the ignoble Tigellinus was deep in Poppaea's confidence, and often called upon as a companion in Nero's orgies, the older commander found himself passed over and at times—although not by his own soldiers —apparently forgotten.

Thus it was easy for Tigellinus to arrange a swift and almost invisible passage, under guard, from Poppaea's house to that of Octavia. There was a grove of trees, there a hedge: and from the hedge it was only a step to the shelter of the garden wall, on the other side of which Octavia habitually sat of an evening. The autumn was advanced and the wind from the Apennines sometimes chilled the nights, but in the late afternoon the sun was still burning aslant the city from some Tyrrhenian brazier in the west, and the small garden where Octavia sat, with every breeze excluded, caught whatever heat there was and held it motionless in the crucible, so that not a leaf trembled or a flower bowed its head. The garden was also removed enough from the house, by means of a long walk under an

ing? Did you not think that he sang for one, and for one only?"

"He sang for love, Lady," Ismene said. "Perhaps it is love for one—I do not know. Perhaps there is no other love. But I have heard nothing so beautiful in years."

Poppaea turned to Tigellinus.

"Do you hear?" she asked him. "Do you understand? This is even more worthy of our attention than I had supposed yesterday. It is enough to put the singer's—ah—possible rivals, if there are any, into a passion of fury. Ismene, you may go now."

To Tigellinus, after the Athenian's departure, she said: "Let it be done exactly the same way, in *exactly* the same way I tell you, tomorrow at the same time. That is, if the Lady Octavia is not obliged to some other duty, if she is free to sit in her garden and listen to her paramour."

The scorn Poppaea was able to put into an expression like "the Lady Octavia" was as powerful as it was delicate, and involved no distortion of her lovely features.

"She is free tomorrow, to my knowledge," Tigellinus contributed.

"I will ask Caesar to go and listen as I listened today," Poppaea said slowly. "I hope I am right. I think I know the result."

She paused, thinking, pulling her cloak about her shoulders. They were seated in the atrium of her house, above the steps, and the evening air had begun to cool after the departure of the sun.

"Some years ago it might have been different," she said, as much to herself as to Tigellinus, "but now I think I can be sure."

The prefect looked at her inquiringly. She felt an impulse to be frank with him: he was her indispensable collaborator at this moment and there were things he did not fully understand, perhaps because he had not been long enough on the Palatine.

"There was a time," she explained, "five or six years ago, when Caesar's response to such a singer as this might have been quite different. He might have become infatuated with the boy, freed him from slavery, enriched him with money and jewels and houses—all of that—and wept endlessly over his singing. Such things have happened, did in fact happen. But now that he has himself competed as singer, as actor and as chanter of verses in so many public competitions, and gained so many medals and prizes, he thinks of himself as supreme in these matters. The Master of the World cannot have a rival. Did he not gain the first prize in Athens and everywhere else in Greece? And in Naples, too? What a bitter affront Octavia puts on him by owning, as slave, a better singer and lute player! Do you begin to see, Tigellinus?"

"So far as I shall ever see it," he replied, "I can see it now. Of course it is not in my comprehension how the Master of the World can care so much about singing. But since it seems to be a fact, let us use it. I shall carry out your instructions."

He was by now so involved with her—so deeply in her debt as well—that she had no fear of neglect on his part. Her immediate task was more subtle than his: she had to make Caesar curious to hear the slave Eucaerus without ever once insinuating that this Eucaerus might be, indeed, equal to the Emperor in talent. She had to hint and cajole, and then retreat from the subject altogether, only to return to it later on in another connection; and all this without once casting the slightest doubt upon Caesar's right to be considered supreme in his art. What she must convey into

than Poppaea in matters which interested her, as Caesar had learned by experience, and yet he accepted such broad statements without a qualm: they were, indeed, the language of the court, compact of mendacity and pretense.

"Tigellinus!" he called.

The prefect, standing a few paces away, was at his side immediately.

"How long has this wretched Greek slave been at Octavia's feet, drooling his drool—?"

"He was bought for her household from the market at Neapolis or Capua a few weeks ago, and she found him when she went to Campania last month."

"Enough," Nero said, as if in pain. "In fact, too much."

He turned again to Poppaea; Tigellinus withdrew again out of earshot.

"Too much to be borne," the Emperor said. "To leave the greatest singer in the world for a wretched half-taught boy—! It hardly seems possible."

Poppaea took heed of the notion, new in all conscience, that Octavia had "left" Caesar, but her lovely face showed no surprise; she could remain attentive but expressionless for long periods of time, perhaps because in reality she did feel very little.

"I will not endure it," Nero said. "She has flouted me. He cannot even sing correctly! Those cadences . . . Like a beaten dog. She has not a scrap of taste. And she never had any real knowledge. What madness, that marriage! For she, anyhow, is mad. She must be, to prefer a weeping, sniveling slave to the Master of the World. I have won upward of eighteen hundred prizes in the most difficult public competitions, and I know whereof I speak. This bastard slave has not the rudiments of his art."

"I felt the same, Caesar," Poppaea told him in her most soothing voice.

"As a poet I have been obliged to carry the weight of the past," Nero said, his voice rising with his anger. "Every fool who can read or write throws Horace and Virgil in my face, and Propertius and Catullus and the rest, not to speak of the Greeks. I have no reply except to point to my published work. But in singing and recitation—well, you know that I have proved myself over and over again, not in Rome alone but in Neapolis and in the Greek cities, and in Athens itself. Nobody ever won so many awards; the exact number is eighteen hundred and eighty; I can show them to you; you were present when some of them were gained. I know what I am talking about. And this puny, pale-faced slut, the daughter of Messalina—of Messalina!—takes it on herself to choose a nameless rat of Alexandria, a whore and whoreson slave, an ignorant, puling dog! They shall learn. She must go at once. At once. And he—well, Tigellinus will know what treatment he deserves. . . . Poppaea, is this the slave of whom you have spoken to me? The one she takes to her bed?"

"The same, I believe, Lord," Poppaea said, stretching out her sympathetic fingers to touch his. Her object, she was now sure, had been attained, and the less she said from now on the better for her cause; his rage would feed on itself with no assistance.

So Piso, revolving in his somewhat bewildered mind the prospects put before him by the conspirators, was driven to think of himself as a "Caesar," even though he had no conceivable connection with the family which originally bore that name. The emperors of the Claudian clan, as he reflected, were in blood just as far off the Julian line as he was; they had come into it by intermarriage and adoption, but they were of no real kinship to the Dictator Julius. This one—the fifth, Nero—had a descent from Augustus through his mother, it is true, and to Mark Antony and other heroes of both sides, but Roman law did not authorize family claims through the female line, except for testamentary property.

Thus he pondered and excused himself from those more practical preoccupations, the how and the where and the when, which absorbed the time and ingenuity of the conspirators. Some of them, notably the young men and the soldiers, were not long in growing cool toward the idea of Piso, whose hesitations and well-bred prejudices aroused their contempt. They were the ones who would have to strike the blow when the time came; they would bear the primary clash of arms; they would die if Tigellinus were quicker to strike than Rufus; without them Piso was nothing. And yet he seemed to be daydreaming in his gardens, parks and orchards, setting the furniture of his mind in order, at a time when every arrangment, down to the slightest detail, remained to be made.

The knights Subrius and Sulpicius, who had been the first to approach Piso, were among the first to experience a disillusionment in him as leader. Their commander and patron Rufus tried to make them see that a more precipitous advance on the road to power would be foolhardy if not fatal; the whole thing required time and caution; Piso was right to avoid firm pledges and irrevocable positions. Rufus, who was not the most fervent of Piso's admirers, found himself defending and extolling the noble Roman for hesitant stipulations which to the young knights seemed to show timidity at least, if not downright cowardice.

The truth they all felt, although none said it aloud, was that Piso's main qualification for the supreme leadership was the absence of competition. There were few who could even be considered for so exalted a task, and of those few most were disqualified by age or some past disability (scandal or feuds in the Senate) which could become an insuperable obstacle in the hour of choice. Against Piso, enormously rich and of great lineage, there was nothing to be alleged except a certain looseness of private morality, which, in Rome, no longer counted. It was therefore lucky, according to Rufus, that they had been able to obtain his consent, however grudging, because without him they would have been headless and without purpose.

"I do not see it like that," Subrius Flavus told him sturdily. "I tell you frankly that I would prefer the old philosopher. The people respect him."

"Seneca? He is sixty-seven—and we may all have seen men of sixty-seven who could do it, but can he? He is older, far older than his years. In these last months he looks eighty or more."

"He has every advantage from the point of view of the public," Subrius Flavus obstinately said. "And we know from the past that he can govern. He has already done so. The eight years during which he was most powerful in Rome were the only years of decent administration that anybody can remember. Even if it is only for a year or two—"

"You discount his death then?" Rufus asked, amused.

"Poetry?" he said. "Do you mean those tirades for the theater? It is not what I call poetry."

"Well, you see," Rufus pointed out quietly, "there are matters in which you and your uncle do not agree."

"Oh, many, many!" Lucan was quick to admit. "Our tastes are not the same. I cannot take to all those long, solemn discourses on pity, and clemency and justice and all the other virtues. Nor yet on the worthlessness of the world. I think the world could be quite a decent place if men permitted it to be. A decent world is even within possibility—within reach. That is why we formed our association, is it not?"

He took a long draught of the good wine from the hills. Sulpicius intervened.

"I don't quite understand you, Rufus," he said. "Do you mean that this disagreement of taste about—well, about poetry—means—?"

"I only wanted to show you that the uncle and the nephew do not think, talk, write or act in unison," Rufus said in a wry, dry voice. "They are not as one."

"Indeed not," said Lucan eagerly. His sparkling eyes and vivid expression in face and voice made him attractive in spite of his lean, awkward body; it was easy to see that his successes at court had not only been in poetry.

"My uncle is an old man," he went on. "He has the ideas, essentially, of half a century ago, those of the time of Augustus. I do not say they are not good ideas, but times change."

"He counts with the people," Subrius brought forth again, "more than anybody."

Rufus amplified. "These worthy knights," he said, "have been thinking that if it came to a choice they would rather see Seneca in Caesar's place than Piso."

"*Seneca!*" the young poet echoed. Evidently he had never really thought of such an unlikely development. "What—what an extraordinary idea—!"

"You yourself said he would be with us when the time came," Subrius pointed out.

"You gave your word, when you went to see him for us on the Via Nomentana," Sulpicius added fiercely.

"Yes, yes, I said he would be with us, I said he was in fact with us, I said he was too old to pledge exactly now, but that I had no doubt . . . Yes, I said all that. But I did not think of the possiblity that he might himself be Caesar."

"The younger associates—these are not the only ones— think that even if Seneca only governed for a year or two and then were forced, by age and infirmity, or in fact by death, to give over, it would still be enough to establish a government and give confidence to the people and the Empire."

This was Rufus, presenting the case with which he did not agree: as he had previously defended Piso against the young, now he spoke for the young in the opposing sense. It was his object to be fair, but in actual fact he only goaded Lucan into more downright statements.

"I don't agree," Lucan said, his whole face alight with honest excitement. "You've misunderstood him. Maybe he was once a noble republican, full of virtuous ideas, but now he's too old and too rich, far too rich. And I even doubt his republicanism, to tell you the truth. He has been making a hero out of Cato right through the years when he was serving Nero, the fifth and worst of the Caesars, and I don't see the sense of it. He would never be, as we are, determined to make the Republic work again. We want a government by the Senate and two consuls with an Assembly of the People and a Tribune of the People. That's what

ciates, everybody who plays a part in our plan, and find out who is the chosen *dux*. To get to the hour of decision without this would be madness. So let us each consult his own friend or friends and let the results be known here, to me, for lack of a better center, and we can go on from there. No doubt we all would like a more glorious leader than we are likely to have—we all would prefer Cato, perhaps Brutus—but we must resolve upon what we have and stick to it."

The young knights, taking this for a dismissal, were soon gone, but Lucan lingered for a little while.

"You have information, prefect," he said, "which is not given to all of us until much later. Tell me, if you can: what is there now—I have heard only the merest rumor—about the Lady Octavia?"

"She is going," the prefect said heavily.

"Ah, the poor lady! There will be anger in the city."

"It will not help her. She has incurred his rage in some way or other. I believe there is some intrigue of Tigellinus in it. That foul whelp, no doubt with the help of Poppaea, has arranged it all. I have heard, only an hour or so ago, that her slaves are packing everything she possesses, including carpets and stuffs and embroideries and such, everything, for a departure tomorrow. There have also been arrests. And there will be the torture chamber for some of her slaves and friends."

"Poor lady, poor lady."

"She might have resisted, if she had been clever—she might have formed a party. Many are well-disposed to her. But she is not clever. She has the innocence, in this place, of a country child. I do not know how it is possible but it is true."

"Perhaps simply to remind the Romans," Lucan said in an undertone; there were tears in his eyes. "They have forgotten innocence."

Rufus grumbled along for a few minutes, mainly about his hated co-prefect Tigellinus, and then found himself questioned again by the young poet.

"Epicharis?" he asked. "Yes, I know her, but not well. I was taken to her house once by a friend. I am not, as you might call it, intimate."

"I was wondering which of our associates might be, well, intimate enough to be indiscreet with her," Lucan said boldly.

Since the departure of the two young knights Rufus had been walking up and down beside the table. Now he sat down again, suddenly and rather heavily. He was a handsome man in his early forties, with a body which had been kept thoroughly in trim, but this heaviness or weariness of his movements seemed to come, like the dark accents of his voice, from some inner trouble.

"I have hoped," he said slowly, "that they could keep the women out of it. Does Epicharis—know anything?"

"Something," Lucan replied, "something, but I am not sure what. I cannot—really—be sure."

He was conscious of deception; he ought to admit frankly his own part in the matter and how much he was responsible; but in his youth and uncertainty before this notable personage, co-prefect of the praetorian guard, he did not dare. It suddenly seemed too monstrous to tell.

"I wondered," he added lamely, "who could have told her anything."

Rufus drummed on the table before him.

"She is not a vestal virgin," he said savagely. "It could be

VIII

By ARRANGEMENT with Tigellinus, who was no longer in a position to deny her anything, Poppaea was enabled to listen from concealment while Octavia's adherents were put to the torture. She did this not only because she was vitally interested in the outcome, but also by taste and desire, because she liked such exhibitions of suffering—just as, when she had brought about the death of an enemy, she liked to see the severed head as a proof. Nero, who understood her predilections, had gratified her in this respect more than once.

But her pleasure with Octavia's slaves was brief and

transitory. Most of them admitted nothing whatsoever—
nothing that could contribute in any way to the story of
guilty association with Eucaerus. Poppaea herself hardly
believed the story and hardly troubled to try: the girl was
"too cold," as she put it, for any passion however secret;
but it had always been an axiom that anybody would confess anything under torture (especially about somebody
else!) and this was the outcome Poppaea awaited in vain.
Eucaerus himself, obviously adoring the princess, would
not gratify the torturers with a single word that could be
twisted against her. He was so obdurate, indeed, and often
so silent even in his extreme pain, that there seemed at last
no use in pursuing the questions. He was sent away, crip-
pled and in chains, to rot away another week or two of life,
until Nero ordered his death for adultery and treason.

The two girls, Claudilla and Domitilla, were even worse.
They screamed insults at their torturers, at Poppaea
(whether they knew she was there or not, and at times
they seemed to know it) and at Tigellinus, particularly at
Tigellinus. The pain of the rack seemed not to affect their
temper but to make it more violent. Even for Tigellinus,
who had a thick hide, their words were often hard to bear,
particularly under these conditions.

"My lady's whole body, every part of it, is more pure
than your mouth!" Claudilla screamed at him when he
asked her a prurient question.

"You are not fit to carry out her slops!" Domitilla would
yell.

Indeed by these insults, the expenditure of rage that
went into them and into the screams with which they were
delivered, the two loyal girls vented that agony which consumed them under rack and screw. Their exemplary
bravery had quickly leaked out; it was the talk of the

Seneca, indeed, would never have admitted the testimony of slaves under torture. All evidence elicited by torture was suspect in his eyes; the evidence of all slaves was suspect; when the two were combined he could put no faith in the result. He had studied all sorts of schemes to curb the institution of slavery itself, which was rapidly choking the life of the governing classes in Rome. He tried to abrogate the old, barbarous laws under which, for example, if a master were killed by a slave (even accidentally) all the other slaves of that same master were put to death, as presumptive accomplices. This horrible law had entailed the death of one hundred and fifty men, women and children, house slaves of a certain patrician, only a few years ago. Men of intelligence and foresight, like Seneca, had opposed the savage sentence but in vain. The most they could do was to save the slave laborers on the country estates of that same patrician from a similar fate. Even the most rabid upholder of ancient Roman law could hardly maintain that these unfortunates, hundreds of miles away, had anything to do with the crime being so direly expiated in Rome.

Seneca had made several attempts to render the actual condition of slavery more tolerable, although it had never occurred to him that the institution itself might be shaken or abolished. Slavery was part of military conquest: you killed in battle and enslaved the survivors, regardless of age or sex. The slave markets grew up upon a basis of such conquest, and as a result an enormous population lived in legal servitude (bound by law) although there was nothing to distinguish them externally from their masters. The slaves were, of course, sometimes of alien or mixed races, but so were their masters; and they were sometimes uncouth barbarians, but this, too, was often true of their masters, particularly among the commanders from the legions. There were highly educated persons among the slaves, poets and philosophers and musicians, and indeed the Greek newcomers who influenced Roman culture often arrived in slavery (although frequently set free afterward). No stigma rested on an emancipated slave, a freedman; his son had all the rights of a Roman citizen; the poet Horace, favorite of the Divine Augustus and of an entire age, was such a citizen. Freedmen grew rich, for commerce was open to them as to few of the Roman upper classes; they married their daughters off sometimes to nobles; they had luxurious Roman houses and country villas of extreme splendor, for no sumptuary legislation held them down. The entire institution of slavery had so waxed in importance, and had so overgrown every part of civilized life in the reigns of the first five Caesars, that, in objective fact, none would have dared to attack it. The transformation of central and southern Italy from regions of small-farm holdings into great estates was deeply involved with this great extension and development of slavery; it was by slave labor alone that such enormous properties could be made to yield a profit; and this constantly rising demand for agricultural bodies created the huge slave markets of the south.

Even the Romans, however unconscious of the larger and slower processes of their history, could not avoid the suspicion that they were gradually being stifled by the numbers of their own slaves. It was most anomalous in that the number was, so to speak, invisible—the slaves were dressed exactly like the masters, cut their hair the same way, were generally clean-shaven like them, and were generally not inferior to their masters in speech, language or manners. Since master could not be distinguished from man, especially when they wore the same clothes (Nero, for example, never wore anything twice, and all his clothing went to the slaves), the confusion seemed to some minds beyond reason. Thus there was introduced into the Senate, some years earlier, a law which would have made the slaves wear a distinctive form of dress inside the city of Rome.

The law had influential supporters—among them, it was said, Seneca. But an alarm, set up by an old but astute Senator, stopped it in time.

"If the slaves wear distinctive dress," this alarming argument ran, "they will be able to see how numerous they are and how few we are. Do we want that?"

Less than a century had passed since the great slave rebellion of Spartacus, in the time of Pompey, which had formed a real army out of the slave barracks of the south and ravaged the entire peninsula for two years. The Senators could not remember it but they had it well in mind just the same. They refused to pass the law for special slave dress.

Seneca had spent his childhood at Cordoba in Spain, where luxury was even greater (for the conquerors anyhow), and slaves more numerous, than in Rome. He was not by nature or temperament fitted to undertake anything that went against the institutions and the laws; he wanted to justify them, rather, by good use. The abuses he saw wherever he looked in Rome had never shaken his belief that the state was good and only its exponents bad; he could have had *Senatus Populusque* carved on his heart; he was by instinct a Roman citizen in that in the main lines he had never dreamed of anything better.

"If the poor lady is to be condemned on the evidence of

a few slaves, only a few out of all the many she had, and if those few slaves spoke under the torture which had no effect on most of the others, she is not guilty and should not be condemned."

Thus Paulina.

Paulina, Seneca's wife, was much his junior and had not yet had time to read all of his works, but she had the dignity and decorum—if not yet the authority—of a great man's wife. Like others of the ilk, she said "we" when she really meant Seneca alone—"we think" when she meant that he thought this or that—and in addressing any third person she never allowed it to be supposed for a moment that any cleavage of opinion, however slight, was possible between them. She was in her mid-forties and a majestic figure when she chose to be; at the imperial court she had held her head as high as the haughtiest of the matrons, and her cloak was encrusted with jewels; but now that adversity had come she was proving herself loyal, submissive, tactful to a degree amounting to special talent, and endowed with all the domestic virtues of most use to her present situation. She did not undertake tasks beneath her rank; Seneca would have noticed and deplored, or at least been hurt in his self-esteem; but those household cares which she could direct she did with a zeal she had never shown before, so that every detail in all their houses was more present to her mind than ever. She never asked awkward questions; she knew that in due course, after he had reflected long enough, Seneca would tell her all she needed or wanted to know; and she did not burst forth unnecessarily at Caesar or any of his favorites. At times, quietly and almost as an incidental accompaniment to talk, she would characterize Nero or Poppaea or Tigellinus, in particular, with words which needed no emphasis, but this was not often. As a rule she ignored the imperial court, at which they had spent the past decade and more, as if she had never heard of it. Paulina had been married at twenty to the philosopher-poet—long ago that seemed now, in the time of Tiberius, indeed only a month or so before that Caesar's death—and had not dreamed, in her modest young womanhood, of the extreme wealth and power to which Annaeus Seneca would one day attain. She had shared the vicissitudes of his rather stormy life, all except the exile to Corsica, from which Caligula's edict excluded her; and she had never for one moment doubted his perfect innocence in that affair, which, according to court gossip and Caligula's evident belief, involved amorous dalliance with a lady of the imperial family. Paulina did not, in fact, see her wise, didactic husband, more than twenty years her senior, as a romantic lover climbing balconies by night; in their childless marriage, to which she had given every devotion, he seemed much more like a father. For this or other reasons she, who knew the morals of the imperial court thoroughly even though she never held them, was unable to believe Seneca guilty of the crime for which he had been sent away from Rome, even when, years later, he had once, in a moment of tender familiarity, hinted to her very broadly that the charge was true. She laughed at his effort to tease her; she knew that her Annaeus was no seducer of imperial dames; she had the kind of belief which is independent of evidence. Likewise she knew that in the present disaster, which to her was not purely disaster since it meant that they could live quietly in the country, all the wrongs were on the side of Nero and Poppaea. Essentially, cutting straight through all the other circumstances—and who is to say she was not right?—she saw it as the will of Poppaea, of Poppaea rampant, Poppaea determined to crown her own voluptuous sexuality as the symbol of Roman sovereignty, her body queen of Rome as no woman's ever had been.

Seneca was more pleased than otherwise at Paulina's staunch belief in Octavia's innocence; any other attitude would have been astonishing under the circumstances; but it warmed him, somehow, to feel the sincerity of her indignation and the depth of her pity. Everything she said in defense of Octavia was, in some way or other, in defense also of him—or, if not defense, at any rate in his favor. He had not actually made the marriage between Nero and Octavia—that was Agrippina's work, in the year when Claudius was away in Britain and the boy Nero had been for a while Prefect of the City—but he had not opposed it. He thought that a closer connection to the Emperor Claudius, such as this marriage to his daughter, would be good for the boy Nero, at that time only fifteen. How was he to foresee that the boy of fifteen, sexually premature in every way, would frighten the bride, a mere child and his sister besides, into a fatal frigidity? For that was, as Seneca understood, exactly what had happened, and he had done his best to air the idea that frigidity was, in young virgins, only a guarantee of virtue. He had never succeeded. As he knew quite well, Octavia remained to this day, at least so far as Nero was concerned, a virgin; and Seneca was willing to stake a great deal on the likelihood that she would live and die a virgin. In these ten years there had been nothing to his knowledge—and he knew a great deal even now: in his days of power he had known everything—nothing to indicate the contrary.

On the terrace in the evening, up in the Sabine Hills, it was so cool that Paulina and Seneca wrapped themselves in their cloaks to sit there, and yet they preferred it because they were out of earshot of the household. Most of their own people, slaves, freedmen and salaried citizens, had been known to them for years, and yet in this day of informers it was impossible to tell who might be making reports to an agent of Caesar. Somebody in the household, some two or three bodies, must inevitably be employed in this manner; Seneca was sure of it. He knew very well what kinds of information reached the private cabinet of the Emperor; he had dealt with it himself for several years, never wholly accepting the validity of anything that came from such sources. And yet—and yet—it was the system. He could believe or disbelieve, but this kind of secret information was indispensable to the rule of the Caesars. They thrived upon their knowledge of their enemies. The whole invention, the principate, was such an amalgam of legality and pretense, old words and new powers, that some such private power was essential to keep it going, to endow it with unexpected strength in the hour of trial and to nip off dangerous enmities before they could flower.

So Seneca, listening to Paulina with a feeling of warmth for her loyalty, was yet compelled to look through the cypress trees to be sure nobody had approached the terrace.

"Perhaps this is all true," he said, "and I tend to believe it myself, but it might be best to say so only when we are sure of not being overheard. I do not know which of our own people are Caesar's spies but I am sure that some of them are."

"It is a dreadful thought," she said. "They are all friends, all tested and true."

"Some may have hidden faults, or even have committed crimes in the past, on which Caesar's agents can play at will," Seneca said. "It is sad. And also it is true that money will do a great deal, and no matter how much money I may pay them, you know that Caesar can pay more. So let us accept it as a condition of life that we are never really alone. Somebody is watching. In this case, at this moment, it is my hope that nobody is listening."

"We are too far; they can't hear," she said. "Oh, how I hate it all! Sometimes I wish we had never lived at the imperial court. If you had been teaching in some provincial capital, Athens for choice, but anywhere—Alexandria, Narbo, Tarraco—we could neither have risen nor fallen, but stayed as we were, which was good enough. And we then should hear of such evils as this, the fate of the Lady Octavia, only after a long time, and very dimly, so that our hearts would not be wrung with sorrow and our minds stunned with indignation. Such things come to the provinces with a thick layer of unreality upon them; they do not seem ever so immediate as they do here; they are hardly believed. We could have lived in that manner. But it was hardly possible once we entered the imperial precincts."

"It started with my father," Seneca said thoughtfully and a little sadly. "I, too, have sometimes thought of what life might have been elsewhere. I could indeed have taught. I might have written better plays, thought more clearly, enlivened young minds. And all this terror of—well, terror of death, for that is what it is—which is the main characteristic of life on the Palatine, well, it wouldn't have existed at all. . . . And yet, Paulina, I am not sure I could have been satisfied. It is too late now for me to separate the strands, but I think there is ambition in me and a desire for power, perhaps also for wealth. Else how did I come by them? I must have wanted them, although with the strength of mind I repudiate the idea. The mind, you see, is not everything. There are other depths."

"There are depths beyond depths in any human being," Paulina declared as if she had just discovered it. "I have known Octavia as well as most people did at court. I never felt any tremendous attraction toward her because she was always so cold and silent. But I knew she was feeling and suffering—I could hardly tell how much, or what—and I think she did believe that I had sympathy for her and with her. Now, of course, I do not believe one single word that has been said against her in these—ah—proceedings, whatever they are, which are to divorce her. I do not believe the story of the Greek slave. It is an obvious fabrication. And yet there *was* a Greek slave; he *did* sing to her in the presence of her women; he did so habitually, every night or almost, and she took great pleasure in it. All that seems to be established."

"Well?"

"Simply this: I did not believe she could be susceptible to music and poetry. I did not think she would listen to one young man day after day, enjoying it. I did not believe she had so much feeling in her."

"She did seem as if she were not altogether here, in this world."

"I am glad she had that little, however little it was, of human attachment or awareness," Paulina said vigorously. "I know it was entirely innocent—no perjury under torture could change that fact—but it was at least some touch of emotion, some heartbeat, that I never expected that poor sad girl to have in life. I thought she was sealed away forever."

"Nobody is sealed away," Seneca told her, rousing himself. "I may seem to be, for one, but at any moment, at any moment I tell you, the messenger may come. This is what I live with."

"And so do I," said Paulina quietly. "When I think of poor Octavia I think also of you, of me, of all of us. This is not a time to live in."

The principal steward of the Sabine household came across the long terrace to bow before them.

"Two from Rome," he said, "want to speak to you. I have told them that it is already late but they insist."

"I should have their names," the old man said.

"Subrius Flavus and Sulpicius Asper, and they come from Rufus, the Prefect of the Praetorians."

"They can wait in the atrium," Seneca said.

He put out a hand toward his wife.

"It can be nothing very serious," he said. "Rufus is a friend. I do not believe he would disturb me for nothing either. These men, whoever they are, mean me no harm. Will you be calm and wait?"

"I will," she said. "It is not my fault, altogether, if I quake and quiver every time anybody comes from Rome. I will wait in my own room. I know it is foolish of me but I shall wait for you to tell me what it means."

"Wife," he said, "it is nothing."

He walked across the long, flat terrace with her and saw her to her own room. Then, going back through the smaller sitting rooms to the atrium, he came upon the two young knights from Rome.

"Do I know you?" he asked, coming forward.

He was very tall, clean-shaven and draped in the white toga, but his eyes were now blazing from a circle of shadow and his face was gaunt from privations. He looked his full sixty-seven years and more.

The young men rose.

"You may not know us, sir, but we know you," said

Subrius, the elder. "Our friend Faenius Rufus has authorized us to come here and speak to you. We are not very
notable persons and it is most unlikely that anybody has
noticed where we have gone."

Seneca smiled ironically.

"In this household," he said, "there are plenty of spies."

"We know it, sir, but we also think it is unlikely that
they could know us."

"Your attendants," Seneca remarked, "will see to that.
But no matter. You are welcome, since you have come so
far and since you come from Faenius Rufus. I hope he is
well?"

"He is, sir, and sends best greeting. This is my friend
Sulpicius Asper, who is associated with me in everything.
This is the signet ring of Faenius Rufus which is, I think,
known to you."

Seneca looked at it and sighed.

"I know it, I know him, I know his family," he said.
"Speak what he has told you to speak."

"It is difficult," Subrius said slowly. "I hardly know
what comes first. Your nephew Lucan has informed you of
an association we have—among the younger men that is,
and with a few of the older ones too—to bring about some
changes?"

Seneca's long hands trembled a little as he readjusted his
toga.

"I know what Lucan told me," he said. "I also know that
I told him I would have nothing whatsoever to do with
it."

"He had the impression," said the bold young Sulpicius,
who had not yet spoken, "that you would be with us when
the time came. He told us so."

"I do not know how he could have had such an impression," Seneca said frigidly. "I know, and I told him, that the secret powers of the prince are greater than any other in the state and that nothing can be kept secret."

"We have come to ask you one thing, nevertheless," said Sulpicius, headlong. Perhaps because he did not believe the old man, perhaps because of the long journey from Rome, he was reckless.

"Say it," said Seneca.

"We believe, we the younger soldiers, that in the critical hour that is coming, perhaps soon, perhaps in two or three months, the praetorian guard should proclaim you emperor."

Seneca groaned as if in pain.

"You cannot say it," he told them. "It is the ultimate treason. My life is forfeit."

"Perhaps it would be forfeit anyhow," said the young man, drawn to the cold sincerity of the old one.

"Yes, that is true," said Seneca. "I often think that it is only a matter of hours. I am well aware of the disposition of our master. But if you think—in madness, in utter madness!—that I might take over all the powers of the state, with the name of Caesar and the title of Emperor—then, truly then, my life is forfeit. I shall die for treason, and it is honestly the one thing of which I have never been guilty."

"I ask you, honored sir," said Subrius, "whether your own life or death is the only thing to be considered in this matter."

"It has some importance for me," Seneca replied.

"Yes, but not so as to rule out everything else. The welfare of the state is the highest good."

"Perhaps. I have sometimes even doubted that. But what

makes you think that government by me or in my name would be in any way desirable when, as I understand it, you have done away with what we have? I am old and tired."

"Let that be. The people know and respect you. There is hardly any other person in the whole of Rome who is thought to have the public good at heart. They all think you have. Therefore, when we have cleared the space of power, we ask you to step into it and govern."

"I cannot and will not," Seneca said with the utmost decision. "Understand it. Believe it. I have had some inklings of your plan, some idea of what you hope to do. I have urged you to give it up—that is, I have urged others of your associates. I keep on saying that you do not know the powers of the principate and how hopeless is your endeavor. I will have nothing whatsoever to do with your plan."

Subrius coughed.

"Do you think, sir," he said delicately, "that this will make any difference?"

"How?"

"Do you believe that if we fail—if our plans become known to the prince and all his powers—there will be any mercy for you?"

"No. Neither in that case nor in any other."

"But then, if your heart is with us, as we all are persuaded, why should you not come with us?"

"I do not believe in your plan. I know too well the powers of the state. And anyhow I am no Caesar. Believe me, I could not at any time assume the supreme power. I have too many afterthoughts, too many compunctions. Do you not understand the difference between a philosopher and a man of action? I obscured the difference myself by acting, during Caesar's minority, in his name. I was wrong. My place is in the study, with the books."

"But you and you alone," said Subrius, "have authority in Rome."

"Authority," said Sulpicius almost on suspended breath, so intensely did he feel it, "and dignity. Dignity and authority."

"These are not power," Seneca said.

He passed his emaciated hand over his closely cropped hair and tried, wearily, to explain.

"Perhaps Cicero had authority, in his exile," he said. "One thinks so today, from his letters. And yet—and yet—who obeys authority? Nobody. What they obey is power. They might listen to Cicero or read him thoughtfully and even painfully, but they obeyed Caesar."

"We are asking you to combine power with authority," Sulpicius declared. "It has been done."

"Not for quite some time," Seneca reminded them. "The Divine Augustus had both, it is true. Since then naked power, violence, and for the most part injustice, have ruled the state. Where do you find dignity and authority? In the pontiffs? In the vestal virgins? In the schools of philosophy? Nowhere. There is nothing left but force, violent force."

"This is what we ask you to assume, to take over," Subrius said. "Combine it with that authority which . . ."

"No, no and again no," Seneca said swiftly. "I will not even discuss such an insane proposal. If you involve me in it, yours will be the responsibility before mankind. I have refused and always shall refuse any implication in your plans, any part in what comes out of them. No doubt I shall die for it just the same. I am prepared. I have been prepared now for some months to die at Caesar's word. But I will not conspire against the state, however degenerate, and I will not conspire against the prince, and I will not accept any office or dignity which might come out of such a conspiracy if it were by any chance successful. Is that clear?

"I hope I may offer you gentlemen a lodging for the night. You are very far from Rome and it is cold in these mountains. I think we have everything you may require."

"We have arranged, honored sir," Subrius said. He was rather subdued now. His friend Sulpicius, red in the face, was on the verge of tears. "My own relatives have a villa not far away and we shall go there for the night. It is best for you, I think, that we should not stay here. We take our leave, honored sir."

IX

POPPAEA'S PREGNANCY had been visible from an early stage, more as a matter of policy than as physical requirement. Her enemies said she accentuated it cleverly, so as to be able to demonstrate at any moment her claim to the marriage honors. She did not go abroad much in the city, partly by preference and partly because she was much disliked by the street crowds. Therefore she was under no obligation of shame or decorum toward the Roman mob; and as for the imperial court on the Palatine Hill, it was already so riddled with shame and estranged from decorum that her condition did not excite unfriendly comment—

nothing, in fact, but congratulation. For this was, in fact, the first pregnancy attributable to the Emperor—the first clearly imperial pregnancy for a very long time—and as such it stirred the ribald wit and frank envy of the Palatine.

However, it was not the Roman pleb or the palace that concerned Poppaea. She was concentrated upon Nero himself, and it was to influence him that she made much of her advancing condition.

"The heir of the Caesars," she said, pointing to her abdomen (in which some said she wore a cushion), "is to be born without honor, while the child of the Greek slave inherits?"

This sort of argument, however absurd, formed part of Poppaea's attack upon Nero, who was well aware of the true situation. There was no question whatsoever of Poppaea's pregnancy, just the same, and his desperate anxiety to have a child—perhaps merely to prove the possibility, perhaps for imperial reasons—made it possible for her to make all sorts of charges, however incongruous.

He could not, just the same, divorce Octavia upon such grounds. Evidence, even under torture and even from slaves, had been too feeble to stand examination. He had already sent Octavia away; the best advice he could get was to divorce her for something less obviously false than adultery. There were no easy crimes of which she might be accused: for example, desertion would have been, as everybody knew, impossible. For Caesar to send her away and then accuse her of desertion was something the Romans, of uncertain temper throughout this affair, might well refuse to accept. It was resolved to put the divorce upon the simplest physical grounds, difficult to prove or disprove, that the lady was incapable of bearing children. Since no attempt had (or so Rome believed) been made to put this thesis to the proof, it was as absurd as all the other charges, and perhaps even more illogical, but Nero at last decided upon it as the solution least likely to cause trouble in the city. He did not know at any time how utterly friendless Octavia really was; he kept imagining powerful combinations of patricians who would come to her aid, or uprisings of the plebs, but if these were to come (and if they were in part caused by the memory of Octavia) it was too far in the future to be of any help to her.

Actually the laws, customs and habits with reference to both marriage and divorce were, and had been for a century or more, extremely lax in Rome. In practice there was no formality; either party could obtain divorce by asking for it; property rights were preserved, the wife resumed her dowry; remarriage was common and frequent, so much so that the matrons of the empire "married only to divorce, and divorced only to remarry," as large a number of times as they wished, and the tie was anything but binding. Aside from this general social condition, Caesar's will was, in practice (regardless of legal theory), superior to any law. The punctilious manner in which the matter of Octavia's divorce was handled, the effort to find unimpeachable grounds for it, arose from the special conditions. Octavia was the daughter of the Emperor Claudius and had suffered much; her brother Britannicus had been beloved of the people; she was herself the object of much sympathy; the easy and quick methods used in other cases might be dangerous here. To this was added Poppaea's nervous fear that something might go wrong at the last moment to impair the legality of her marriage and the rights of her child.

"The law? The law?" Poppaea would say to her women and sometimes even to her men. "What is the law? I have no use for it. It has never been of any use to me. Why must I respect the law? Is Caesar to obey the law?"

And yet, in that tremendous, awe-inspiring golden net which caught the whole of Rome, she did not dare deny it.

"You, Caesar!" she would say to Nero. "You have the right of judgment in the imperial court, the one and only, the court of treason. You and you alone. What else is law?"

She arranged her tears so that they fell, globular and distinct, between her globular breasts.

"Am I to be the victim of your Roman law, your Roman law, your Roman law?

"That incredible old bore Seneca said he did not know what the law really was," she told Nero. "If he did not, who did? And then there the even more incredible old bore Cicero. Thank God I never knew him. My youth has given me some advantage. I never knew Cicero. I render thanks to all gods that I never knew Cicero. Seneca was bad enough. The worst I ever knew. The worst, the worst. Caesar, if you rule the world, give me a diadem. Give me no law. Give me a diadem."

"Woman, there is no diadem in Rome."

"Caesar, I want a diadem. Do you behold in your own person the most exquisite youth in the universe? Do you know yourself to be the most desired of all wondrous human bodies, the most admired and beloved? Golden one, it is true, or it has some element of truth, but I must tell you that before I saw you there was my Otho, the stalwart truth of Roman manhood, the one who . . ."

There was generally some rude altercation or inconvenience at this point, because the handsome Otho (whom Nero had loved before he even knew Poppaea) was always a difficult subject. What Nero did not know, indeed, was that Poppaea had urged her preceding husband into the imperial bed, in order to extol his wife, and that it was by this indirect but deliberate method that Caesar had learned of the scientific skills of Poppaea. The exact mechanism was not known to the Emperor, and yet there was that one subject—the beautiful Otho—on which he could never be at ease. It was like the subject of his murdered mother in a lesser category: Agrippina could not even be mentioned, and every thunderclap or streak of lightning made him tremble at the thought of her, but Otho—who was still very much alive, and flourishing, as an idol of the legions and governor of Lusitania on the far coast of the Atlantic Ocean—came next.

Nero, as he considered, had much to suffer.

But Poppaea in her advancing pregnancy thought that her lot was almost unimaginably worse. She was Poppaea Sabina (Sabinus was one of the grandest senatorial and consular names). She had been married and divorced various times, it is true, and had opened her body to almost everything in Rome, but she never for a moment forgot the immensity of her lineage—nor did she yield, at any time, to the passions she satisfied. A cold but voluptuous woman, vicious in the sense of vice, she had discovered political ambition in her mid-thirties and had used it. She was a decade older than the Emperor but that was a detail: she was now pregnant by him, an achievement none of the other ladies on the Palatine had even dreamed upon, considering the Emperor's habits, and she would by means of this pregnancy become the Emperor's wife—that is, Caesar's wife—and perhaps have a temple dedicated to her, with hymns and incense. Moreover, she would have jewels such as no other woman in Rome ever had, and incense, incense, incense even outside the temples.

Poppaea valued all this, but most of all she valued power. By power she meant principally the power of life and death, the severed head and the truncated, abandoned body. She had come to value the "power of Caesar" because she had found the joy of vengeance. She did not want to build or make anything at all. The power of life and death meant chiefly the power of wielding death, savoring and appreciating death. This was her desire. Caesar's insane passion for building, making, creating and doing—in which he was as far outside intelligible life as she—was not within her comprehension. She did not know why he wanted to create. She did not even know why he wanted to have a child, but by her infinite skill in sexual exercises, having understood what he wanted, she arranged it so that he could do it, and, as a result of enormous sums given to the leading astrologers and necromancers of Rome, it eventuated in a pregnancy which, Poppaea thought, would settle everything.

The Emperor was twenty-five and she was thirty-five, and if she could only marry him in time her child would be legitimate and would inherit the earth. That is, naturally, if it were a boy. Never did it occur to Poppaea or anybody else that it might not be a boy. The entire expectancy of parturition referred to a boy. Indeed it was not the custom to pay any attention (publicly or privately) to an imperial pregnancy unless it had some reference to the succession, the strangely improvised and uncertain succession to the throne of the world. Augustus, who never had a son—and his great-uncle Julius Caesar, who never had a son—may have expressed their longings in a form of adoption, but it did not provide the Empire with any safe or secure method of passing from one reign to another. The Fifth Caesar of the Julian-Claudian house, the last of the family, having done his full share to exterminate the possible inheritors of the earth, was now in a fever to create his own successor: Nero wanted a son of his own loins, child of his semen, as no member of the family of Augustus ever yet had had. If he had murdered that son soon afterward, as he might well have done, he still would have wanted that son.

Poppaea received all that she could of the complex and essentially weak world-wish of Caesar but translated it after her own style: *she* wanted a son and it was *her* son who would rule the world. This had nothing to do with maternal love. She had sons by preceding husbands and paid no heed to them; one, indeed, was murdered by the whim of Caesar's jealousy and she was calm. But her imperial son would be imperial: that is, he would have total power over the known world. This was something quite intoxicant to the Roman mind, worse than wine or the poppy seed. A Roman empire subject to the rule of law, going along in a jog-jog fashion without the slightest regard to the scandals of the Palatine or the intrigues of Rome, was a reality—it was indeed a reality then and for centuries—but from the point of view of Poppaea it had no existence. She knew that Nero was the last of the Caesars, the last of the house of Augustus; she was to produce another, the continuer of the line, and this would be the Caesar of Caesars; she wanted nothing, nothing, to impair the radiance of his birth and deification. She had already exacted from her husband (who was weeks away from being her husband) the promise of deification, and for herself the honor of Augusta. There was nothing she did not call down upon the head of the unborn boy. God-children were common at the time in all sects, even some obscure ones, and Poppaea had determined in advance that she would miss no point in her calculation.

And thus it was that Octavia was thrust from the south to the islands and then to death. Actually, under Roman law, her divorce was quite irrevocable. She had no friends and no recourse of any kind. Caesar had decided. But he had decided only, at first, upon her divorce, and this upon the ground of barrenness. She was then sent in custody of some praetorian guards (in the command of Tigellinus) to the southern seacoast near Neapolis, where she was embarked for the island of Pandataria, and there, friendless and alone, was put to death.

Her death was not necessary even for Poppaea's marriage. The Roman divorce law was by now so accommodating that it would have legalized almost anything, and besides, there was no longer any power in the magistrature or elsewhere in the state to question Caesar's will. Octavia had been divorced. Caesar was free to marry. But Poppaea was so anxious to prove to all future generations—and above all, for her son about to be born—that she was actually and legally Caesar's wife, that nothing short of Octavia's severed head, brought to Rome for her delectation by the order of Tigellinus, would satisfy her. That horrid sight, which confirmed her vengeance and her coming triumph, was reported in the city in spite of the precautions of secrecy, and added to the growing horror with which many Romans regarded Poppaea and all her works. She was saved from any open show of disrespect by her habit of seclusion and by the fact that just now, when her marriage had been at last assured, she chose to retire to the country for a few days so as to make a more solemn return to the Palatine.

The ceremony of marriage had seldom been so unnecessary. Roman law would have regarded Nero and Poppaea as already married—one year of living together continuously was enough, and they had been together for five years. But the ancient laws had fallen into disuse, and in any case Poppaea wanted augurs and omens, priests and astrologers, to dignify the occasion. So it was ordered and done, although without the public display which might, under the circumstances, have irritated the mobs of Rome.

"So we are about to have a really royal court in Rome," Faenius Rufus said to Lucan in the seclusion of his own garden. "That is what she wants and will get. Pomp and ceremony, obsequious forms, new fashions from Asia. I regret to see it happening, of course, but it only changes the outside of things. Inside, beneath a few remaining Roman forms, everything has already changed. We are under a despotism of the most extreme kind. We might as well use the words 'king' and 'queen' and be done with it."

"I doubt if we ever fall so low," said Lucan furiously. "And I for one would not wish to live if it happens. So long as there is still some slight remnant of old Roman form —about the Senate, for instance—there is still hope. I don't agree with you that the forms don't matter. I know they are only external. I know that underneath the pretense of a republic we are now the slaves of a tyranny. A worse tyranny than any Oriental king ever enforced. But I still would keep the forms if I could, in the hope of bringing them back to life."

"It does us little or no good to prefer anything," Faenius Rufus said. "Our preferences do not count. The Senate itself is able only to obey Caesar's wishes. Do you realize, Lucan, that if we are not able to go faster with our plans, it may all be too late? I have heard that there will be new coins, with Poppaea's head on them alongside of Caesar's. The child that is to be born may be—I think will be—given immense honors at birth. We may face the day when a child, even an infant, will be our sovereign. As happens in Oriental countries. And with the real power in the hands of Poppaea and her friends. Such things have become possible. We have gone a long way from the Senate and people of Rome."

The little groups which, in an expanding circle, formed their conspiratorial society talked in this fashion with an ever-increasing gloom but in fact did nothing more. Much of the movement, if it could be so called, depended upon a leadership which was at best reluctant and at times lacking. A clear order could not be given and there was no certainty that the separate groups understood their own tasks in the general plan. Rufus might have commanded, indeed, since he had both training and authority, but he was held back by the personality of Piso, who did not seem to have a distinct or continuous idea of what he wanted to do. There were days when Piso counseled inaction, delay, further reflection; there were other days when he wanted to enroll new and dangerous elements; there were times when he seemed to regret that he had even tentatively accepted a predominance for which he had no gift. These were handicaps in the eyes of the more ardent conspirators, who found their desire to move forward constantly frustrated by alternations of caution and distrust. If they could have found another illustrious Roman of wealth and ancient family they might even yet have gone to him instead of Piso, but the suitable candidates were few or completely out of reach. The whole plan seemed to sink into a sort of marshy terrain of the mind, a climate of indecision.

To the woman Epicharis this seemed worthy of contempt.

"Romans indeed!" said she. "You chatter like a courtyard full of Egyptian slaves and meanwhile the time speeds away. I am willing myself to do something, anything within my power, and there are things, but you tell me to be quiet, to say nothing, to do nothing, until the order comes. I believe that if you wait for Calpurnius Piso there never will be an order. He is the weakness of your plan. If you could have reached Plautus in time—but no matter; he is dead, too. The urgent thing, I believe, is to get started, either with or without the knowledge and approval of Piso. If he withdraws afterward, no matter. There will be somebody. We can call on a number of these noble Romans once they see that the danger is over. I want to talk to my friends at Misenum."

"No," Lucan said, weary and worried. "That is what you must not do. Above all, Misenum. But essentially what you must do, dear Epicharis, for me and for all our friends, is to remain silent, discreet, loyal. It will be for just a while longer. The moment Rufus gives the word I will tell you."

He had discovered, not all at once but by an occasional slip on her part, that Epicharis was on terms of intimacy with no less than five members of the secret councils known to Lucan. He was not horrified for himself; no idea of fidelity had entered his mind so far as Epicharis was concerned; he assumed she had many friends; but it was alarming to discover that so many of them were privy to the schemes centering around Piso. In the present state of delay and confusion the one important thing was to keep Epicharis from talking, and to this the young poet addressed himself with all the skills he had by nature or art. She was fond of him, fonder perhaps than of some others— he was younger than almost any man she received—and her cultivated mind rejoiced not only in the fact that he was known and widely accepted as a poet, but also (he was obliged to believe) in the substance of his poetry itself. At least she could quote it by pages and often referred to it in ordinary conversation, so that he could not in common sense reject the hypothesis that she had attentively read it. Whether this had preceded or followed their relationship he could not accurately determine, since she had begun such references almost from the time of their meeting. Any woman in Rome could have done the same: Lucan was most famous, he was imperial in favor and fortune, and the women of Rome, whatever their station in life, were always well aware of the heights whereon Caesar dwelt. But the idle snobbery of awareness was not the only flattery Epicharis knew; she could say the words themselves; and the fine flower of her flattery was that she could also say the words of his illustrious predecessors. She quoted Virgil and Horace, Propertius and Catullus, with the same grace and ease, and often she would do him the dizzying honor of quoting him at one moment and one of these the next, as if they were a brotherhood of seers and familiars, the tutors of her heart. He was on his guard against everybody and everything, and had learned from his earliest childhood the dangers of surrender. He was, even now, only twenty-three, and had been the favored nephew of an all-powerful minister since his tenth or eleventh year. Even so, the arts of Epicharis, a woman at least fifteen years his elder, did not fail to entrance him both in the body, which she knew as a musician knows his instrument, and in the regions of the aspiring soul, the Stoic spirit, the web-weaving imagination, wherein no other woman in his experience had entered with sure and comprehending tread.

As a result, instead of obtaining from Epicharis full reports on what she knew of the conspiracy, and from whom she had obtained her knowledge, Lucan was imparting to her, bit by bit, and half knew that he was doing so, everything that he knew. The sluice gates were working the wrong way. He was not constantly or completely aware of what he was doing. At times he only realized a few hours or a day after he had left her how much he had unfolded; sometimes he did not know for a week or so; sometimes he never took it all in. She did. What with what she could glean elsewhere, which was not negligible, this astute and deep-running woman came in a few months to be in possession of every tangible or comprehensible fact about the great conspiracy against Nero. Its ramshackle structure and its lack of coherency made her long to take charge, to organize and command; she felt the fearful dangers into which these foolish men were wandering; she desired above all things what they also desired; and the obligation to be silent while they wasted irreplaceable time was testing the outermost edges of her control.

"If I were more than I am," she would sigh, "if I were one of you! I am only a woman, a poor woman, an ordinary woman, although a Roman woman. Who am I to tell you what to do?" And then, ferociously: "What right have I to tell you that your friends and leaders are no better than donkeys and geese? If I were a rich noble with countless ancestors, like Calpurnius Piso, you would listen to me, even though I had the brains of a small bird! I tell you to strike at once, and if you do not, you are lost. Poppaea will soon be in absolute power. Poppaea will be

Empress, even though you do not like either the word or the idea. She will be Empress. And if she ever has a child whom she can put on the throne of the world she will do so. You think Agrippina was ambitious? You do not know Poppaea. She will rule at any cost, even if she has to kill Caesar and do it in the name of this bastard she is about to foist upon us. I know Poppaea better than any of you do."

And, try as he could, Lucan never discovered how Epicharis came to know Poppaea at all, and so much better than the men who frequented the Palatine. Perhaps she only meant that, as a woman, she understood Poppaea better than any man could possibly do; but he thought it was something more, much more than that—some bitter-sour experience, some untoward encounter, in which the lascivious lady of high degree had aroused the hatred of Epicharis. It seemed too personal a hatred to have its origin in the patriotic passions which moved the others.

Whatever it was, it gave Epicharis an edge of urgency in her talk, a weight of intensity in her manner, which could not but impress Lucan and even frighten him a little, not physically but in his poet's imagination.

Worst of all, he reflected—and repeated to Rufus—was that Epicharis had echoed, in different words but with no essential difference of thought, the warning Rufus himself had given: that Poppaea intended to rule, even if it had to be through a child. Rome had never yet undergone the experience of regency, although Nero's accession at the age of seventeen came near to it: Seneca had preserved the state from Agrippina's ambition and had forced her to keep hidden behind a curtain when she insisted on attending councils of government. The idea of a wanton strumpet like Poppaea governing the Roman Empire was new, strange and horrible. To Lucan it would have seemed simply laughable if it had not been so impressively brought forward by both Rufus and Epicharis, both of whom, in ways he could not guess, and before he had been himself fully aware, must have known Poppaea to the depths.

There were many others in Rome who lacked such direct knowledge and yet had come to very nearly the same conclusions. Nero remained popular, even now, because of the large sums of money and quantities of foodstuffs he gave away, as well as for his absurd desire to show himself as actor-poet-singer before the general public; the Romans had indeed had fools for emperors (the memory of Caligula was green) but had never before had an emperor who wanted to play the fool for them, specifically for them, and for their capricious applause. They had the sensation of being wooed by their own dictator, which was novel and flattering, especially since he gave them more free grain and games (gladiatorial combats, animal shows, baths, parades) than any of his predecessors.

But none of the Fifth Caesar's friends and courtiers had an ounce of popularity left by the time of his marriage to Poppaea. Poppaea herself was detested; her henchman Tigellinus, Prefect of the Guard along with Rufus, was regarded as one of the lowest of criminals; here and there in the court there were men whom the mobs regarded with friendly amusement, notably Petronius, the "Arbiter of Elegance" as Nero called him, a fop and wit of the most dazzling courage both toward the dictator and the pleb. Rome admired Petronius and even had some affection for him, especially after his indecent novel (the *Satyricon*) began to be widely circulated among those able to read, though it was much doubted that he had himself written it. There was an enormous respect for Seneca; it had very sensibly increased since his removal from power and from

Caesar's presence. But the horrors of the past decade had by no means vanished from the consciousness of the people, and however badly or wrongly told, they were told over and over again: the murder of the Emperor's cousin and adoptive brother Britannicus, the rightful heir (if there were such a thing in a dynasty without a constitution) to his father Claudius, a woeful deed, a beautiful boy only fourteen years old, to whom Nero before the murder offered "the final insult to his budding manhood." Then, the murder of Agrippina, the Emperor's mother, after several attempts defeated by her energy and acumen. Wicked though she was (and the imperial women were all supposed to be supreme in varieties and intensities of wickedness, as they generally were), she had sacrificed for the son who murdered her, and had indeed murdered her husband (uncle) Claudius to make way for him. To this, just now, so recently that no Roman tongue could name a date for it, had come the horrid murder of the innocent Octavia, the pale, pure girl brought up to be Nero's sister and then imperially thrust into his marriage bed. Britannicus and Octavia, the beautiful boy and the exquisite girl, were the nearest thing to ideal or romantic presentations the house of Augustus had offered the Roman people in a dreadful half-century. This brother and sister, who remained alive in the popular imagination, may have been associated with other ideals already existing in the myths of the state religion; as victims they beclouded the brightest moments of Nero's reign; as realities they had been known and loved (even though dimly and afar) by countless Romans and visiting Italians, and even by the strangers—from Gaul, from Spain, from the province of Asia—who came at stated intervals to the capital for business and pleasure.

All of this had made its mark on the Italian mind, which

may be subtle enough to forget but is also tough enough to remember. Nobody on the Palatine cared very much about Italy, which had been considered part of Rome for the past several decades. Catullus was an Italian born in Verona, outside the Roman borders; so was Virgil, of Gallic origin; so was Horace, whose father, being a slave and probably a prisoner of war, no doubt came from the province of Asia or one of its neighboring kingdoms; Italians were almost the same as Romans by now, or at any rate the Roman citizenship had been extended to them all. Outside of Italy was the Empire, to which the denizens of the Palatine during these precise months paid no attention at all. The Empire ruled itself, according to a consistent empirical structure evolved during the preceding two centuries, with the proconsuls and legates from Rome presiding over a system of tax-collecting, troop-recruiting and magistrature which for the most part was administered by local authorities. Imperial and commercial necessities (such as road-building) were the constant care of Rome; so were important ports; so was peace between the parts of the Empire and on its borders. The alien and barbarian powers, although far away, were a constant preoccupation in that their appetite for loot, if nothing else, tempted them to perpetual raids upon the valuable peace-built wealth of the Roman provinces and dependencies. The legions were disposed so as to defend the provinces on well-marked lines (the Rhine, the Danube, the Euphrates, among rivers; the desert below the Nile in Egypt). At this point the legions were almost entirely Italian. The admixture of barbarians, although it had begun, was in its early stages, and when Nero referred to a "Spanish legion," for example, he meant simply an Italian legion stationed in Spain.

To Poppaea and to many other luxuriant flowers of the

Palatine Hill none of this had any reality. The Roman Empire scarcely existed for those who made the most of it. Nero himself, although he had been most carefully trained for government by one of the wisest tutors any prince ever had, was insecure about the geography of his realm. His concentration upon poetry, declamation and the theater gave him a most natural inclination toward Greece, which he knew well and where his efforts (in Greek) were applauded. Aside from Italy and Greece it is doubtful if he knew the disposition of the Empire, where he had never been and of which the maps were so poor. The stories he heard of the cold forests in Britannia and Germania, with their bloodthirsty inhabitants, gave him no desire to go there, and the Gauls seemed to him, with their somewhat higher organization for opposition when required, less picturesque but more dangerous. Like all Italians, he was content to be where he was, so long as the world paid him tribute.

In other words, Nero and Poppaea were very nearly unaware of the world they pretended to govern. In Asia Minor alone there were at this moment provinces, allied kingdoms and dependent states with individual characteristics unknown to the Emperor. There were, starting at Trebizond on the Black Sea, Pontus, Paphlagonia and Bithynia, Mysian Phrygia, the Roman province of Asia, Lydia, Caria, Lycia, Phrygia, Pisidia, Galatia, Lycaonia and Cilicia. Beyond that, Cappadocia, and below it, Syria. Beyond the slightest doubt Nero had been made to study the map and the history of all these states in his youth—Seneca was a taskmaster—but it is a certainty that he knew little about them.

He was safe in the assumption that they were Hellenic or Hellenistic in culture, Roman in justice and administration of the law. Outside of this broad, general statement, which applied to everything in the legacy of Alexander (everything from Macedonia to Egypt), there was nothing the Fifth Caesar knew of his world in the east, nothing at any rate to show that he knew. His extravagant reception of King Tiridates in this very year shows above all things his desire to be hospitable to an Oriental barbarian who carried with him (in his Chaldean astrologers) the secrets of destiny, the decrees of the stars.

For, little as Rome knew of the Empire, the Empire was creeping in upon it like a fog. The Palatine, the hill where the Caesars dwelt, was above the fog, perhaps, or so it was thought—that was the principle of its foundation.

And yet it was hardly possible to walk for ten minutes through the marble corridors or formal gardens of this palace area without encountering some sort of astrologer, necromancer or ordinary magician from outside of Italy. The Italian augurs told fortunes in the ancient, familiar way by the entrails of a chicken, a partridge, etc., etc., and by the flight of a bird and the sunlight on a thicket. The astrologers from the Orient, many of them by way of Greece and by this time many of them actually Greek, were concerned with the relations between the astral firmament and individual men. They believed (or said they did) that every event of any consequence in human life was determined in advance by the influences obtaining between the heavenly bodies and the living creatures on earth. Within fifty or sixty years they had obtained the most absolute belief and obedience on the part of the rich Romans (the poor had not yet heard of them). Tiberius himself, although skeptical by nature, at least toward his own official religion, was a slave to astrological determinations and kept his great astrologer Thrasyllus with him to the very end on Capri. It was a son of this Thrasyllus who now dominated much of the thinking at Nero's court. His name was Balbillus, and the Emperor (perhaps from fear?) never forsook him.

The doctrine of the astrologist was that although all man's fate was predestined (as the Roman official state religion proclaimed), this was because of emanations connecting the heavenly bodies, chiefly the seven planets, with the lives of human bodies in their brief dance on earth. It was not, of course, possible to overcome fate or destiny (*Fortuna*). It was more implacable than any concept known even to the Greeks. But, since it depended on relations between the stars and men, if stars in their movements were studied profoundly enough, it might be possible to arrange the deeds of men in time and space so as to deflect the ire of destiny—so as to make these magnetic effusions less baleful and occasionally even to make them favorable to an enterprise of man.

Do it Tuesday at eleven in the morning, not Wednesday at four in the afternoon.

Beware of next week.

Do not take a journey in the month of March.

If the sun shines, wear a blue dress.

The calendar—the calendar not read, seen or understood, but interpreted—was the rule of life.

Poppaea and Nero, neither more than the other, believed the astrological statement far more than they did the statement of the official religion. The religion gave them fate; astrology explained fate. Thus they became, like most persons known to them, concerned not so much with fate itself as how to escape it—most of all, by their Chaldeans, they hoped to defeat the stars.

X

To DEFEAT THE STARS is presumably easier with a resident astrologer, assisted by a staff of wise men, in constant attendance. Even so Poppaea was obliged to wait twelve days after Octavia's divorce before she felt it safe (or her advisers felt it safe) to risk the permutations and conjunctions of the heavenly bodies.

Then, without public parade but with due attention to every augury and portent, Poppaea was wedded to the Fifth Caesar and retired with him for a space to the country. In this interval of their legal bliss they did not impose too much too suddenly upon the Roman people, but as the pregnancy advanced, and Nero more precisely anticipated the pride of fatherhood, he could not resist a few manifestations. For one thing, he put Poppaea's head on some of the imperial coins in profile alongside his own, and since he had excellent coin designers, the result pleased even his captious eye. Such an honor had no legal basis—and indeed the principate, based on the command of the legions, had no room for women; Caesar's wife was that and nothing more; but Augustus himself had made his wife Livia into an Augusta, with divine honors. Nothing less would satisfy Poppaea, as became quite clear during the next few weeks.

What the terms "Augustus" and "Augusta" meant in custom, law and religion was mercifully vague, and had been purposely left so by Caesar Augustus. The terms had overtones of the official state religion, and the first Augusta was deified; she also had immense wealth and an unimaginable influence over the reigns of her husband and son; but she was never called "empress" and never exerted any special power distinct from that of Augustus and Tiberius. There was no doubt, just the same, that "Augusta" was the highest term the Romans had for the highest honor they could bestow on any woman, even of the imperial house. It was therefore Poppaea's desire to attain that honor as soon as possible—or any other that would make her position more secure.

Nero was in somewhat less of a hurry. His daily reports from Rome, which were in the main from hired informers (the kind of professional spies called "delators"), made him well aware that his marriage had not itself been popular and that Poppaea was only a trifle less vilified in the public report than she had been before. As an aftermath to the disgrace and death of Octavia—about which several successive rumors, most of them highly unpleasant, had swept over the city—the Emperor himself was at times the subject of tavern jokes of a bitter nature, as well as of some rhymes, generally indecent, which circulated among the people. He knew these things because the informers could not possibly coördinate and reconcile their reports; in the main they did not even know each other; so that if one prudently omitted anything that might displease the Emperor, another was bound to put it in for fear of displeasing worse by suppressing it. Thus, by setting one bit of spy lore against another, Nero came to have a tolerably good idea of the state of public opinion in the city, and he was not anxious to make it any worse.

Thus he resisted, for weeks on end, any effort to make him hasten the honors for his new wife, but at the same time, to spare himself some of her complaints, he was lavish with the gems and gold ornaments, precious embroideries and stuffs from Asia, which were her delight. Toward the end of her pregnancy he consented to one thing: that at the birth of Caesar's heir she should be proclaimed Augusta.

There were some changes—not only apparent but real—in the imperial court after the marriage. Some of Nero's favorite slaves of both sexes retired from court to one or the other country villas belonging to him. Thus Acté, the slave from Asia by way of Athens, was honorably, even luxuriously, accommodated in the hillside villa of Velitrae looking toward the sea. Poppaea's dislike for her might have exacted a worse sentence, but she had learned that she could not obtain everything at once, and Acté could wait. Some of the other slaves were scattered about the countryside so that the new Augusta (to be) would not be obliged to see them. For a time, although nobody could have expected it to be permanent, the legalization of his concubinage with Poppaea seems to have given Nero some idea of changing his ordinary life, reducing it more to the dignity and decorum of the house of Augustus. Such notions, which centered mostly about his approaching fatherhood, could scarcely be more than whims in a nature like his, nor would Poppaea herself have relished any real return to the manners and morals of the Augustan day. While it lasted, they played at it; it was a convenient make-believe for the moment, and had the additional advantage of novelty.

Another notion which appealed strongly to Nero was that his heir should be born at Antium, where he himself had seen the light twenty-five years before. Thus when the mild winter descended, he and Poppaea, with their courtiers, guards, astrologers, ministers and throng of all their clients, not to speak of the medical men and surgeons and midwives now in attendance, moved to Antium. He had been born there as the child of Agrippina and Ahenobarbus (and in no sense as heir to the Empire) on December 15th, on which day the court now celebrated his twenty-sixth birthday.

And there, beside the sapphire sea, and with no trouble or discomfort in the doing of it, Poppaea gave birth on January 21st—but to a girl.

Her own fury was great, and there was considerable disappointment at the court and in the city. The anticipation of an heir for the Empire had restored Roman equanimity just during those weeks, and the first news of a girl-child was not welcome.

Nero changed all that because, curiously enough, he was delighted with the child and evidently paid little attention to its inability to rule over Rome. He had quite possibly doubted, up to the last, that the child would ever be born; he may have doubted that he and Poppaea were capable of such a miracle; he may have feared death or disability for one or the other, mother or child. Whatever his reasons, he burst into joy and ordered all the conceivable celebrations, fireworks and free grain, parades and temple offerings, to mark the birth. The newborn girl (Claudia by name) was proclaimed Augusta at once, and at the same time Poppaea was elevated to that dignity. She and her daughter were the first since Livia Augusta, wife of Divine Augustus.

All these events found the half-organized conspirators at Rome in their usual state of talkative discontent. A fear was growing among them that Poppaea's ambitions might bring them to a worse pass than Nero's extravagance, cruelty and corruption. They pointed in dismay to the fact that a small infant had been proclaimed Augusta, along with her mother, and that if such an unprecedented thing meant what it seemed, it constituted some sort of vague threat of female rule in the principate. Rome had never been ruled by a woman and for centuries had considered any such rule as being characteristic of the weakest Oriental despotisms. Nobody had yet forgotten the visit (more as conqueror than as conquered) of the beautiful Queen of Egypt long ago; there were even people still alive who could remember how she dominated the Dictator Julius in his own capital.

The mere idea, therefore, that by making the new baby Augusta, Nero and Poppaea were indicating a possible future, even a conceivable future, was enough to strike most Romans with horror and deep foreboding. Their loathing for the monarchy came from ancient days and was deep in the general consciousness; it had been greatly forti-fied by the barbarian kings, princes and queens they had seen, generally as conquered ornaments in a general's tri-umph, and who had (some of them) settled in Rome. When they said "Oriental despot" they were expressing a very real horror, even though what they had under the trappings of the "Republic" and "principate" could not by any license be considered better. Indeed by this time much of what the Romans thought in public affairs had become sheer myth, and even their own vaunted ancestry and racial purity were not to be taken as proved. Greeks and barbarians had been brought in as slaves from the wars of the past two hundred years and more; they had, many of them, been freed and mingled with the rest of the citizens; an Oriental influence in philosophy, social custom and even religion was beginning to be powerful in the whole of Roman life, along with a decline in belief for the old pantheon.

Under such conditions it sometimes seemed ironic to the beholder (such as the enlightened Greek slaves of the day) that the Romans, particularly among patricians, could get into such a passion of patriotic rage over the thought of "Oriental innovations" when the authentic Romanism of the old Republic had long since been worn out and overgrown.

Lucan was a case in point: he was still only twenty-three years old and had never in his life seen republican institutions in control, yet he was as passionate an adherent of the Republic as if he had been born in it. His *Pharsalia*, deflected at the outset by his early friendship for—or adulation of—Claudius Nero Caesar, had become an ardently republican document after its third canto, so ardently republican that it was hardly surprising to see it come under the imperial ban. Other and better emperors might, in defense of the regime, have taken the same steps to suppress that poem. At the time, of course, it was said—and Lucan almost certainly believed it—that Caesar's action arose from deep personal jealousy of a poet who was his superior in the art, and the chances are that the Emperor's motives were mixed. So were the poet's: by now his ardent republican principles, which were sincere enough as worship of the past, were much augmented and even envenomed by a sense of personal injustice, of having been monstrously maltreated by Caesar. He lost no opportunity to present his case to persons who were willing to listen, for he loved to talk and had small liking for discretion: in every respect, one might have said, a poor conspirator. Thus when he had the opportunity to talk to the lame Phrygian, Epictetus, as he had done more than once in the days of his imperial favor, he seized upon it eagerly; it was a chance not to be encountered every day as things stood now.

This Epictetus was a slave, even younger than Lucan, and had been bought off the auction block by Epaphroditus, once a favorite slave of the Emperor and now set free for other—and constantly more important—employment. Epaphroditus, also a Greek, had been much taken by the few remarks he exchanged with this Epictetus, who spoke pure Athenian and seemed to be remarkably clear in the head. In spite of the fact that the boy was ill-favored and lame, and could therefore not be much good for ordinary work, Epaphroditus thought he would be useful as reader, teacher and secretary, since his syntax and enunciation were so superior.

At a period when Lucan was still welcome in Caesar's circle he had met and talked a number of times with Epictetus, whose function in the house of his master had quickly changed into something resembling that of Greek teacher. It was a privileged position—not unique in Rome, but privileged—because there were many on the Palatine, even among the greatest nobles, whose knowledge of Greek was limited and who welcomed the opportunity of a little classical conversation in the pure Hellenic of Athens. Epaphroditus made the slave available to all these great folk as a part of his hospitality in the evening, and Lucan had quickly discovered in him a mind which, although unlike his own, was certainly its equal. Such conversations had ceased, so far as Lucan was concerned, about a year ago; he no longer frequented any of Nero's favorites since his own fall from favor, rightly doubting his welcome.

So, when he found himself actually passing Epictetus down by the Circus Maximus on a day late in this same winter, Lucan put out a hand to detain him and spoke most courteously. Somewhat to his astonishment the young slave, who had never been very cordial to anybody in company (perhaps because of self-consciousness about his duties there), now replied with a genuine smile and eyes alight with friendliness. He made no difficulty about turning and walking with Lucan for a space, and actually remarked, with tranquil courage, that he regretted the ban on the latter's poetry. Lucan, less tranquil, made some bitter remark and then said, impulsively, that he regretted not being able to talk to the young Phrygian any more. To this Epictetus gave such an answer as to encourage an invitation: that he had much time during the day, not many duties, and for instance at this moment would not be expected or required in the house of Epaphroditus for an hour at least. All this in such Greek as gave Lucan delight to hear; for he, too, had been at school in Athens, and his own use of the language was scarcely less beautiful than the slave's. He had in fact hesitated between Latin and Greek as the language for his poems, but had chosen the former as being more widely read in Rome itself, if not elsewhere.

In consequence of all these courtesies and, perhaps most of all, of the language in which they were speaking, the patrician asked the slave to come up and talk for a while and have a glass of wine.

"I should have asked you at once," he explained, "except that there are not so very many persons living on the Palatine who care to be seen much in my company."

The slave smiled gently.

"What have I to lose?" he asked.

They made their way (not far: to the Caelian Hill) talking of minor things and even, for part of the time, not speaking at all. Lucan was surprised at the slave's courage and surprised at himself for being surprised; furthermore, he felt downright grateful. Some such element was probably present also in the mind of the slave, who, although privileged to talk to the noble Romans in groups, had probably never walked through the Forum with one of them before; moreover, one who could speak his own language with such grace. The life of the cultivated slave was bound to be lonely; his equals were of no use for conversation, his master was rather a pupil than anything else, and the noble Romans were more like a class in the academy than individuals. He had not learned that consummate appeal to the mind of a single person which was to make him, in after years, the greatest of teachers; he was still too unsure of himself to be sure of anybody else.

Lucan understood all this well enough to put him at his ease when they reached the villa and went through it to the enclosed garden at the back. It was, of course, rather lavish (money had always been plentiful in Seneca's family), but the slave spent his life in palaces of equal grandeur. It was not gold or marble that could make him uneasy; but untoward circumstances, the awkwardness or even the scorn of other slaves in his presence, the strangeness of a strange house—such things still had power to disturb his equanimity. Lucan's skill in kindness (in which skill was ever difficult!) made such things vanish, and soon they were having their glass of wine under a pergola and talking with greater animation than could have been possible in larger company or other circumstances (in the house of Epaphroditus, for instance). It was the late winter and getting warm; the day was verging on noon; some of the flowers had begun to send out warnings of spring. Lucan, expansive as always, spoke of his suppressed poetry and then of the lack of liberty in Rome today. From this it was an easy move to the Palatine, to Caesar himself, to the recent events and the general ruin of institutions in the Republic. Without heat or rancor, always in the same quiet, amiable manner and the same beautiful language, Epictetus replied, not at length but to the point. All of what they said was not for us but much was.

LUCAN: In many ways the Republic has already ceased to exist but I still value the forms as a means of return. We could still reconcile the Republic with the principate by going back to Augustus.
EPICTETUS: I doubt if you will go back. Things do not. But they do not stand still either.
LUCAN: In that case we are going from bad to worse.
EPICTETUS: Possibly. But change for the better is also possible. Only, it is most unlikely to be a return to the past —it may be better, but a new kind of better, not an old kind.
LUCAN: Do I understand you to have a passive attitude towards all these things? I know that your position in Rome would not make you concern yourself too deeply with our public matters. Furthermore, as a Greek you must must feel yourself a stranger among us. But

intellectually you cannot fail to be interested in your surroundings and what goes on in them.

EPICTETUS: I am interested. Of course. I see and hear a great deal every day. But I am not concerned, not involved, not endangered. This is not merely because I am a Greek slave. That condition may be altered at any moment. Indeed, Epaphroditus has quite plainly said that he intends to set me free soon. I shall still be a Greek, but, to tell the simple truth in this matter, my interest in Rome is great enough to make me want to stay here, and I have told Epaphroditus not to free me until I am a little older and a little more qualified to earn my own living. I am not concerned and not involved, but this is not for the reasons you give.

LUCAN: You can earn a living very easily by teaching, and I am glad Epaphroditus will set you free. But if all this is so, then why do you care so little what happens to Rome?

EPICTETUS: I do care. But not with that passion which the participants show, and which, if you will forgive me for saying so, very often destroys their reason. I care, within reason, for Rome as much, or almost as much, as for Athens. Although I am Phrygian by birth, Athens is my home so far as the things of the mind and spirit are concerned. If Rome is to be my temporary dwelling place, I can accommodate myself to such conditions as I may find. It is not difficult.

LUCAN: It is most difficult for me. I see the whole state overwhelmed by tyranny and injustice, our oldest rights abrogated, the treasury ruined by senseless extravagance, and every citizen at the mercy of a rule without law. Do you expect me to be unconcerned?

EPICTETUS: I do not, indeed. You are, if I may say so, a representative member of the very class which actually does govern Rome, although this class is small in number compared to the total of the Roman citizens. When you speak of liberty you speak essentially of liberty for this small class to which you belong. Is this not the truth?

LUCAN: Perhaps. When you put it like that, I think I must say it is the truth, or at any rate has truth in it.

EPICTETUS: There are far more proletarians than patricians, you will admit, and the slaves have now become, according to my own guess, even more numerous than the others put together.

LUCAN: This may be so.

EPICTETUS: If it is so, then your indictment of the principate as it now exists does not apply to most Roman citizens, slaves or proletarians, but simply to the patrician class, many of whom still govern throughout the Empire, many of whom hold the highest posts out here in the city.

LUCAN: They—we—are the guardians of the institutions.

EPICTETUS: Which you made, of course, and for your own highest purposes. Wait—I have not finished. Aside from this class feeling, that is an apprehension that the Caesars have disregarded the patricians and that this particular Caesar wants to destroy them, you have a personal feeling in the matter. What is it?

LUCAN: I can hardly say with exactness. Your terrible Athenian lucidity has confused me a little, and I am only trying to match it, which is not an exercise I often take.

EPICTETUS: Are you not angry because Caesar has caused your poems to be suppressed?

LUCAN: Perhaps that is part of it.

EPICTETUS: You know, or should know, that it can only be a temporary suppression. This Caesar is not eternal.

LUCAN: He is, however, young and healthy.

EPICTETUS: The poems will survive him.

LUCAN: Whatever I feel personally in these matters is of no great moment compared to my deep sense of outrage at what Claudius Nero has done to Rome. I may resent the suppression of my poetry. I do. I may also resent the indignity with which my revered uncle was sent away from court after eight or nine years of the most tremendous service—more, if you count the years before Nero was emperor. Furthermore, I resent the way in which, after a favoritism which even to me seemed exaggerated, Caesar thrust me out of his house and more or less warned his entire court to have nothing to do with me.

EPICTETUS: These are not great sufferings.

LUCAN: They are not, compared to what may come. It is true that my property, or that of my father, or that of my uncle, has not yet been taken. And, up to now, we have our lives. But I assure you that we anticipate anything, anything, from what now governs us.

EPICTETUS: Go on.

LUCAN: Perhaps I have already said it, but I must say again that all this does not count with me. What counts first, last and always is the state of Rome, which is being destroyed in every institution and every liberty.

EPICTETUS: I believe you. It is the principal historical characteristic of the patricians to care more for the city and the fatherland than for their own lives, wives or children. As I have said before, this is because the city and the fatherland exist mainly to gratify the wishes of the patricians, both materially and in these matters of their high principles. The same patriotism would arise in other classes if they were the beneficiaries of the city and fatherland.

LUCAN: The plebeians have played an enormous part ever since the Gracchi. And Julius Caesar courted them too, beyond all necessity. Nowadays they are more or less guaranteed a livelihood by all these extravagant donatives of Claudius Nero. The poor fools do not realize that he is only giving them part of what he filches from them and from us.

EPICTETUS: True. But the proletarian, who has nothing to contribute to the state but his children, is even lower than the plebeian, and does not always share in the privileges which the Gracchi and Caesar won for the plebs. In other words, you speak for the smallest class in the state and yet you believe yourself to speak for the entire state. Attend: I have something more to say. Supposing the plebs to share your fundamental patriotism, as they have often done in the past—supposing, for example, although it is hard to suppose today, that Rome were actually attacked—

LUCAN: It has happened.

EPICTETUS: It could happen again, but always differently. Supposing it did happen, would you expect the patricians and plebeians together, as in the past, to defend the city?

LUCAN: Certainly. What else?

EPICTETUS: Do you attach no importance whatsoever to the growth of the city proletariat—that is, those with no reserves or resources, who cannot even pay taxes, those who have by legal definition nothing to contribute but their children?

LUCAN: I do not know how numerous they are. I seldom see their part of the city.

EPICTETUS: I believe them to be numerous. But far, far more numerous, by what I see and hear, are the slaves, coming from all the world, from Asia and Egypt, Britannia and Germania and Hispania, many Italians among them, and Greeks and barbarians of every race, thronging the streets of Rome on the errands of their masters. If I do not guess too badly, the slaves outnumber the patricians by a vast proportion—when one man owns a hundred and fifty or two hundred slaves it is easy to see—but they also outnumber the plebeians, most of whom do not own slaves at all except for manufactures and other forms of city work. It is perfectly possible, from what I see here, that there are more slaves in Rome than free men of any category, patrician, plebeian or proletarian, citizen or provincial.

LUCAN: I have not thought of it so. I have only wanted to set the city free again according to my own ideas, which may be those of a single class but have value in my mind.

EPICTETUS: You might find that a very large number of the inhabitants, those with whom you have no acquaintance, actually would prefer Nero's sweetmeats and carnivals to the bitter bread of freedom. That is, if freedom connotes responsibility also, as I gather.

LUCAN: But what do you want? You, the single keen young Hellene of mind and marrow, what will you have?

EPICTETUS: Freedom.

LUCAN: You tell me you can have it when you wish, and that you have asked Epaphroditus to delay it a little.

EPICTETUS: That is not the freedom to which I refer.

LUCAN: What other is there?

EPICTETUS: There is the one of which you speak, which refers to public institutions. But there is the one I mean also, to which I aspire: the freedom of the soul. I do not in the least mind being a slave so long as this condition refers only to my legal condition of body. I want to be free of possessions, as well as free of being possessed. Without house or wife or child or slave, with only my cloak about me, to sleep under a tree and earn my bread by whatever means may come, such as teaching my own language, I could, I think, be happy under any political institutions that might prevail. I must learn to endure and to renounce. That is the only freedom that means anything—and I could achieve it just as well under slavery, just as well under the tyranny of Claudius Nero the Fifth Caesar, as in any other condition. This freedom depends upon me and comes from within.

LUCAN: To endure and to renounce.

EPICTETUS: Endure what comes, renounce what might be.

LUCAN: It is hard. Behold, Hellene, my uncle Seneca has been a Stoic all his years. It is very fashionable in Rome to be a Stoic. I have not noticed that it has diminished his possessions. On the contrary, with every book he publishes about renunciation of the world he seems to accumulate a few more millions and a villa or two in addition.

EPICTETUS: His conditions are different. I do not judge him. You asked me what I wanted and I was telling you.

LUCAN: It would not be hard to attain.

EPICTETUS: On the contrary, it will be extremely hard because it depends on me, it comes from me. I can only be
free in the sense to which I refer by freeing myself of
the bondage of things, of the passion and greed of the
world. This only I can do, but if I live long enough I
will do it.

LUCAN: It is not my desire. But I am a prey to all the
passions.

EPICTETUS: You are a poet.

LUCAN: And you?

EPICTETUS: I aspire toward philosophy. Some day I shall
be a philosopher.

The poet took the philosopher out to the main gate of
the house. This was a very noticeable courtesy from a
Roman noble to a Greek slave, but Lucan did it to be sure
that his guest did not suffer any indignity from the other
slaves he might encounter on his way through the house.
At the gate the owner of the house paused for a moment
and said: "Epictetus, I am proud, rich and passionate. I
shall never be a philosopher. Is there anything you can say
to me?"

The slave smiled his gentle, sidewise smile and spoke
slowly. "I think you exaggerate the powers of Caesar," he
said. "He can take your life, it is true, and your property,
under tyrannical dispositions which may be wrong but
cannot last forever. The loss of life is final; there is nothing
to be said of it. But up to that, in a thousand respects,
Caesar is powerless even in tyranny. Can he give you a
fever? Can he obscure the sun? Can he deprive you of
love? He may suppress your poems but he cannot deprive
you of the power to write them. Let him have his powers,

such as they are, great as they are: there is a more irresistible power inside your own soul."

The young men parted and did not meet again. There was seldom any reasonable excuse for such a meeting, and the events which now crowded upon them made it out of the question, but Lucan, at any rate, never forgot the words of the lame Phrygian. As he walked slowly back toward his own quarters in the house, his mind brought back to him some words in the third ode of Horace, a little like this:

Not the rage of the million commanding things evil,
Not the doom frowning near in the brow of the tyrant,
    Shakes the upright and resolute man
    In his solid completeness of soul.

He was somewhat assuaged, a little calmed down, by this conversation, even though his principles and purposes were in no respect changed. It was the deepest influence of the Stoic upon those who listened: in the turmoil of life there were few who put the words into action, but even to think of them conferred some element of tranquillity. Endure and renounce: these words came often into Lucan's head. So far he had had little to endure and he was in fact renouncing nothing, but the ideas brought up were nobler than the notions of every day.

Those fears, vague as they had been, aroused by the proclamation of the two Augustas—the notions of Poppaea's ambitions and the threat of female rule—were abruptly ended or at least lessened early in the month of May. The child Augusta, the four-month-old baby Claudia, died suddenly and was deified. Better a goddess, the cynic Petronius was supposed to have said, than an empress.

XI

ON THE NIGHT of the eighteenth of July, Seneca was oppressed and more than usually gloomy. He thought afterward that it might have been as a result of some mysterious emanation from the events far away. He was not a superstitious man in the least, and when such things occurred to him he marked them down simply as impressions from an unknown source. He did, however, tell his wife Paulina on that night itself that he had never known such heat in the Sabine Hills, that it seemed to him something beyond nature and outside of climate, and that he felt it must portend some catastrophe—a terrible storm, an earthquake—altogether outside the common experience.

His villa was a good day's ride (that is, by a good rider with horses in relays) from Rome. He did receive messengers from Rome fairly often, from his nephew or from friends, but on the eighteenth and nineteenth of July there were none. The heat was close and humid, and in spite of the thick stone walls of his castle on the hilltop it seemed almost impossible to breathe, even in the vast library, normally so cool and quiet. He and Paulina, having no guests in the house and none but themselves to consult, had their meals under the pines on one side of the garden, looking down toward the Via Salaria. The old man rambled on a good deal about things that had happened a long time ago, as he was inclined to do nowadays, and his wife supplied that minimum of attention which was necessary to keep him going. He spoke of omens, premonitions, auguries and the like, in which he had no faith.

"This heat would be an omen to many," he pointed out. "I even think it might be the sign of some approaching disaster. But in the sense in which our Roman priests use the word, there are, of course, no omens. We use all these things, as we use the gods themselves, partly as a discipline and partly as a satisfaction to the people. If they had no such fear of what is above and beyond nature they would be more unruly than they are. That is why such an immense structure of priestly learning has arisen. The people need priests when they are worried. They need gods when they are afraid."

"Yes," said Paulina, "they do."

"We must worship the whole base throng of gods without forgetting that we do so to set an example, not because they exist."

"Yes," said Paulina, "it is so."

"The sage will always remember that it was we, or our progenitors, who invented the gods."

"Yes," said Paulina.

A slave appeared through the cypress and came over the large, rough stones to where they sat beneath pines.

"One from Rome," he said, "with messages for the Lord."

Seneca as a rule would have told the slave to feed the messenger and tell him to wait. Tonight, because of the close heat and the strange feeling of premonition, he said that the messenger should be admitted to the terrace and give up his message first.

The man appeared—a sweating barbarian who had ridden far and fast in the service of Faenius Rufus—with a piece of parchment in a leather case. Seneca took it and dismissed him with recommendations of good treatment.

He read the message by the light of the hooded candle and then read it again and his hands began to tremble slightly.

"Wife," he said, "we have finished our meal and we may as well go in."

"What is the matter?" she could not help asking. "What has happened now, Annaeus?"

"Rome is burning," he said.

"It would not be the first time," she said with considerable tranquillity. "We both remember a number of times when—"

"Oh, not that, not what you remember, not what I remember," he said. "It is something quite different. A whole, a total fire, a fire all over the city at once, starting in sixteen or eighteen places at once, a fire that must have been set alight by intention."

"How can such things be?" she asked. "Sixteen or eighteen places at once? By intention? Who could want to burn Rome, the whole of Rome?"

"Who, indeed?" he asked, rising.

As they walked to the inside of the castle on the hill he spoke quietly, without emotion.

"The city will burn like sticks of dried wood," he said. "There are huge areas where only the poorest of the poor live, crowded together, and the service for fire prevention is most limited. I did my best to strengthen it in my time but it is still nothing. The whole of the poorest part of Rome will burn and the people will be homeless. The hills will be safe enough—the Palatine, the Caelian, the Janiculum across the river—but the rest will burn like straw. It is a hot and dry time of year. Sometimes it seems that there is a curse upon it."

"But you said," she persisted, "that it started in sixteen or eighteen places at once, as if some criminal had been at work. Who could do such a thing?"

"My message says nothing of that," he replied. "It tells me the mere facts. The fire began on the night before last. This morning it was raging. It had covered ten out of the fourteen regions of Rome by this morning and showed no sign of abating. My informant says nothing of how it happened. He merely says that it was no ordinary fire because it gave evidence of simultaneous origin in many places at once, all over the city."

When they retired to their private quarters Seneca's hands had not ceased to tremble. He sat with the message in his hand and read it over more than once. Paulina watched him in anxiety and fear.

"There will be further accounts given of this," he said after a long silence. "However, I believe that I shall entrust the messenger—the slave of Rufus—with a word for my

) 179 (

nephew, so that he may come here in a day or two and tell me what he knows. It is not at all what could or should have happened in the ordinary course of things."

"The messenger returns to Rome in the morning?" Paulina asked, striving to keep her nervous tremors out of her voice.

"Yes," the old man said. "He will go back. He may as well carry a word asking Lucan to come here in a day or two. I would hesitate to involve the boy in my own disfavor if it were not for the fact that he has come here himself, of his own free will, two or three times since we left the Palatine."

There was another long silence. The slaves had lit a fire in the vast fireplace and both were sitting near it. Curiously enough, the day's heat did not seem to have penetrated these thick stone walls, and even tonight the fire appeared to be a necessity. Neither of them thought of what it might mean, this shiver that made them cling to a fire on a night in mid-July: that it might mean the apprehension of death, the clammy fog of disaster on its way.

"You know," Seneca told her after a while, "there is one part of the character of Caesar which I have never fully understood. It is his desire to create anew that which was sufficiently created before. In other language, he would like to rewrite Lucretius, Virgil and Horace. He is not satisfied with anything as it is. According to his fabulous vanity, which I have never really plumbed to its depths, there is nothing that has been done which he could not do better if he had the opportunity to do it. By this I mean in the realm of works of art, both the written works and the works in marble, stone or paint. I have frequently observed the discontent with which he acknowledges perfection. Even as a small boy he was intensely jealous of Homer and Virgil, because he could not hope to do what they did. He resented every word I said about them. He resented Catullus and Propertius even more, a little later on, because their verses were more akin to his own and more beautiful. He has appreciated many teachers of singing, poetry, declamation and the like, and rewarded them highly, and many Greek actors too, but I never failed to notice that the ones he rewarded the most highly were the ones who most slavishly praised his own efforts."

The old man sighed heavily.

"This was an endeavor beyond me from the start, Paulina," he said wearily, after another silence. "When I came back from Corsica I was filled with joy and hope. No philosopher of my time has been given such an opportunity. Plato himself, in going to Syracuse, had no such hope because his tyrant was already formed, was already in full and sovereign control of the state. I had the chance to create an emperor out of a boy of ten, not a grown monarch. I was conscientious, severe, indefatigable. You know it yourself. But there were some innate characteristics, some deep-rooted desires and evil propensities, which no force from outside could hope to dominate or overcome. He had them from his mother, perhaps, or from his remotest ancestors, or quite possibly—how do I know?—from the stars. Deepest and strongest was this vanity, this insane and Promethean vanity, which makes him want to outdo all men and rival all gods."

Paulina watched the fire. Tears were running over her cheeks, unnoticed, because she was not sure what Seneca meant her to understand by these awful words but she feared the worst.

"My interference with Roman society was never useful, had no results, had no meaning," he went on. "I tried to mitigate slavery and lift the moral code; I tried to make peace more desirable than war, even in the remotest regions; I tried to keep the venality down, the financial corruption at a minimum, the taxes and the confiscations to a bearable level. All these things, and a sort of censorship besides, occupied my days, year after year, while the Emperor was still too young to rule. And it was in vain. What I should have been doing, it seems, was another matter: I should have been attempting to correct the defects of his own nature, rather than those of the state, because in the end, as it turns out, he is the state and more, he is the Empire, the gods and the law. I have done badly indeed."

"You could never have changed him," she said through her tears.

"No doubt that is true," he said slowly. "That makes the vanity of the effort fairly complete in every direction. I did nothing for the state and nothing for the Emperor."

There was a long silence.

"Why do you say these things tonight?" Paulina asked at last. "What fault have you that Rome is burning?"

"Do not ask me," he said. "Let us go to bed. I have failed. I am old now. I know better, but it is too late."

In the morning the messenger of Rufus was sent back to Rome with a brief note saying that Seneca would be grateful, in two days' time or whenever convenient, for a visit from his nephew Lucan. The note did not mention the fire.

On the same evening a messenger arrived, also posthaste (that is, by relays of horses) from another friend, a Senator. There were numerous Romans who still, although paying their court to Caesar, were cautious enough to keep on a distantly friendly basis with Seneca; they were merely assuring themselves against a change in climate. This Senator gave the old philosopher almost exactly the same information as Rufus had done by the preceding messenger, except that he added two ominous details: first, that many had already died in the fire, uncounted hundreds of men, women and children; second, that the city was filled with wild rumors and a kind of rebellious fury at its fate.

This was on the twenty-first; on the twenty-second, two messengers arrived with more or less the same news, and in addition some details about the exact losses of property; on the night of the twenty-third, Lucan arrived.

"I am not exactly uninformed, my boy," Seneca told him. "Some friends have taken the trouble to send me the news, so far as they could. I observe that you did not."

"I was told that Rufus would keep you informed," Lucan said. "He is my friend and promised me. As Prefect of the Guard he has powers I do not have. For the horses, for the roads. It is a very bad time, and no Roman knight or noble can get through without special help. The Via Salaria is crowded."

They were on the pine terrace at one side of the castle wall, and the calm valley fell away below them toward the Via Salaria, which was invisible behind orchard and vineyard. No sign of tumult was there. No more peaceful scene could have been imagined in the late July evening, green and gold. From the lurid descriptions which had come to him Seneca was obliged to look in the west for the flickering reflection in the sky of an immense conflagration, and this even though he knew that the distance was too great; it was as if the burning of Rome must make a larger-than-life effect upon all its surroundings, all Italy and the world. Here was peace and silence.

"I came as soon as I could," Lucan added, rather shame-facedly. "I was trying to help fight the fires. I put all my able-bodied slaves into it, too."

"Your house is safe?"

"So far the fires have been rather far off. The Caelian and the Palatine are untouched, except by smoke. There is smoke everywhere."

"I have even tried to imagine seeing it in the sky here," Seneca said, relenting a little. "You may go to the bath, my boy. You need it. When you are ready, come to me here. I want to know many things, but before you go you can tell me one, perhaps the principal one: is it true that the Romans think this fire was deliberately set alight?"

"Yes, Lord," Lucan said. "They think so. It is hard not to think so, since it sprang up at the same moment in many far-separated parts of the city."

"But who could have done such a thing? It seems hardly credible, hardly even possible."

"Some fifty or sixty men, obeying orders and following a plan, could have done it," Lucan pointed out. "It required a plan, of course, but it shows every evidence of a plan. Every place where the fire began was a place of notable wood and shingle, inflammable in the highest degree."

"Have your bath, have your bath, get the horse from your nostrils," the old man said hastily. "Come back when you feel a little restored." Then, to Paulina after Lucan had gone: "I am afraid of what he is going to tell me. I do not want to hear it, but I must."

It was in this mood that he received his nephew for sup-per on the terrace a while later.

"The baths are small but good here," he said, "and you will be the better for some wine and food. But even so, you can tell me more while you refresh yourself."

Lucan gave an account, rambling and profuse, of the events of the preceding days and nights as he had observed them: the horror of the unimaginable fire against the summer sky, never ceasing, scarcely ever dying down, the remorseless extent of it, the throngs of helpless people struggling to escape from Rome with all their household belongings, the death of whole families in the densely crowded tenement districts of the city. Paulina asked for specific information on the houses of friends, on places known to her, on certain areas where she had often been. As the whole thing became clearer Seneca perceived that his own friends and class—the Senators, consuls, patricians in general—had not greatly suffered, but that the mass of the city dwellers had lost not only shelter but whatever else they happened to possess. They did, of course, occupy most of the city, while the patricians were not only much fewer in number, and chiefly on the hills, but had also the protection of stone and marble to discourage the spread of fire. What was more, most of their houses were surrounded by spacious gardens where the supply of water was kept at a good flow. As in so many other events known to him in a long, busy life, this catastrophe seemed to the old man to fall most heavily upon those least able to bear it. He sighed heavily and fell silent for a long time while Paulina and Lucan talked.

At last he came back into the conversation with an effect as of returning from a distant journey.

"Lucan," he said very quietly. "You spoke of the fire as being set according to a plan, and upon orders. You must have some idea of whose orders this might have been. Do not speak loudly, as we may be overheard, but speak just the same. What do the people believe?"

"They believe what I told you, sir," Lucan replied in a

low voice. "They say there were men with burning brands rushing through the city on the first and second nights and refusing to let anybody use water or any other method of stopping them. I have heard many Romans, freemen, citizens, say that they saw this. I did not see it. I have also heard that when these men with brands of fire were attacked by some of the people, they shouted back that they had authority for what they were doing."

"What authority?"

"Perhaps of Tigellinus, I do not know," Lucan answered. "They say that some of the men of the praetorian guard were among the incendiaries. I have no means of knowing. But it is quite certain that the mass of the people now believe it was all done by order of Caesar, who was at Antium all these first days. He was said to be returning to Rome today because his own house is in danger."

"It could be protected easily enough," Seneca said in the same reflective undertone. "He can have all the water he wants, and his house is all marble, and furthermore it is protected by gardens on all sides. If it is burned it must be because he wanted it to be burned."

"Rome is full of rumors," Lucan said, looking around him at the empty terrace. There were shadows at its edges, beneath the cypress trees; there were shadows at the corners of the castle wall.

"I do not believe you will be heard from here," Seneca encouraged him, "but just do as I do, and keep your voice down."

"Some of the rumors are very difficult to believe," Lucan said. "Caesar is said to have rejoiced at the thought of Rome burning. There is one story to the effect that in his own theater at Antium, to an audience of his familiars, he sang a long poem of his own composition about the destruction of Troy, comparing it to what was happening in Rome. I do not myself understand how he could have written a long poem so quickly, or how the Roman people could know about it. Much of this is sheer invention, I have no doubt, but it shows how the people feel."

"It is not of necessity sheer invention," Seneca said slowly, reflectively, as if he were pondering each word. "Nero may have written the poem first and derived from it the idea of burning Rome. It is well within the nature he has somehow acquired or grown into. Suppose he had written such a poem during recent weeks or months and wanted to give it the most awe-inspiring performance possible. Would not the burning of Rome supply the pretext and in a way the accompaniment? It sounds insane, but I am not at all sure, at times, whether his sanity remains intact."

There was a long silence. Paulina stirred but did not dare to speak. Such talk frightened her profoundly.

"We must all remember," the old man resumed after a while, "that his uncle Gaius Caligula was beyond any doubt subject to seizures of madness. He was sorry, he said, that the Romans did not all have one neck, so that he could behead them all at once. His cruelties were madness; so was his extravagance. . . . Nero is not unlike him, in spite of every effort I could make."

"He may bring upon himself some terrible revolt of the Romans," Lucan said. "They are in the most dangerous mood it is possible to imagine at this moment, and the fire was still going on when I left. Caesar is openly accused in the streets. These things are not discussed in whispers, as we are doing here. They are shouted by many, many thousands of dispossessed, homeless people. Many of them have lost their families as well as all their property. I do not know that Caesar is safe in Rome, if it be true that he is returning there today."

"The praetorian cohorts will see that he is safe," Seneca remarked in a voice heavy and hopeless. "If they are insufficient, he can bring in the legions. They will all defend and support him because he gives them everything they want, and more. He has bought his safety."

"But perhaps not forever," said Lucan. "There are limits to all endurance."

They sat there for a while and drank wine while the moon rose over the hills and the villages in the valley before them went to sleep. It was a scene of peace and virtue but to all three of them there seemed to be another scene somewhere behind or beyond it, the flame and horror of the tortured city where they had lived their lives, long or short, and dreamed their dreams, now never perhaps to come again, of a better world.

XII

THE WOMAN Epicharis was safe enough from the fire because she lived on the Pincian Hill, in a region of tombs and villas, outside the main regions of destruction. She could not, even so, overcome her agitation, fear and anxiety for the first few days, and by the time she had heard all the city gossip from her slaves and those who visited her, these emotions were increased by an overweening anger against the prince whom Rome blamed for it all.

The fire died down on the fifth day, it is true—precisely on July 23rd, the day when Lucan rode to the Sabine Hills to see his uncle Seneca—but took up again with renewed vigor, and perhaps from renewed incendiarism, for another three days and nights. By this time the Emperor's house had been destroyed, which, in view of its nature, seemed to be by deliberate arrangement (it could so easily have been saved); and three entire regions or quarters had been turned to dust and ashes. There were seven more of which nothing but ruins remained. Even the great stone temples of the most ancient days, the relics of the earliest Rome of antiquity, fell before the flames, were looted and smashed to bits. The treasures taken from the temples and other deserted, burning palaces were beyond an estimate. Food ceased to come into the city; the water supply, always better in Rome than anywhere else on earth, failed in many areas; the roads in all directions were crowded with people escaping from the horrors of the world's capital.

Epicharis was by no means a rich woman; she had only seven slaves in all. They were enough to keep her protected and fed during the week of the nightmare. When it was over, and Rome was substantially in ruins, she could survey those ruins, still smoking, from her garden on the Pincian Hill outside them. The revulsion of her soul at all this unnecessary destruction was accompanied by a fierce determination to do what she could against the tyrant who was the cause. Moreover, it would be months or even years before life could return to anything like a normal basis in the city. Epicharis had many influential friends, and therefore sources of supply, but even her house was feeling the pinch on food and other necessities. There was disorder in the city still, after this wild looting and drunkenness. One slave had totally disappeared—not a valuable one, a mere barbarian from Britannia or Germania, but it was an indication of the lawlessness afoot. She resolved to put her cause to an advocate, with respect both to the missing slave and some damage for her garden hedges, and then lock up the house altogether, leaving one old man in charge, and journey south to Misenum.

This would have been a dreadful journey for anybody else in her stratum of Roman society. The rich, traveling with large numbers of slaves and sometimes with horses if they were in a hurry (horses being more costly than slaves), could go to Misenum or anywhere else they chose, fending off the multitude as they cleaved through it. The poor, who traveled on foot and had neither pride nor haste, could get to Misenum or anywhere else because they did not mind the hardships and delays. But Epicharis was neither rich nor poor. She had a certain feminine pride and a fondness for comfort; moreover, she liked to be taken for a lady of importance; and she did not think she could undergo some of the humiliations and abuse which travelers in this crisis were willing to endure.

So she used her important friends without mercy. Many were away from Rome. She could not reach Lucan, who was still in the country with his uncle, or she might have pressed him into service (as she had intended) to accompany her. But there were others who remained in the city. She was happy in the favor of Plautius Lateranus, a consulelect whose powers, greater than his masculine attractions, enabled her to obtain relays of road slaves and an armed escort for her journey. Her own slaves followed her litter on foot, carrying objects of value or utility which she desired to keep with her in Misenum. Among the valuables there were also books (Lucretius, Virgil, Horace, Catullus, Propertius, and with them also Lucan's *Pharsalia*) and a few Greek carvings, for she was a learned woman. The slaves had no trouble keeping up with her litter because progress was slow. The dense mob flowing out of Rome—

not so dense as before, but still a flood—could not be pushed aside even by her armed escort at times. She slept when she could, drew her curtains and her veils, but even so she could not shut out altogether the sight of the misery on the Appian Way. And the heat was so terrible that she was obliged to open up from time to time, so that the whole spectacle was before her, the weary, weeping children and their haggard mothers, the men determined to go onward although they could scarcely put one foot ahead of the other. Every wan face and bedraggled form, every evidence of human suffering, increased her rage against Nero and—as she put it—Poppaea. There were times when she thought of it only as Poppaea, leaving Nero out. It was Poppaea who was to blame for everything.

In Misenum itself she had a little house on the hill with a charming garden, where many of the sea soldiers had been wont to come in other seasons. She ought really to have come to Misenum sooner, because Rome was too hot in midsummer, but what with one thing and another she had postponed her journey. Now, although it took place under the most awkward circumstances, it was just as well that she had not come earlier: her house in Rome might have been burned or looted by the mobs if she had not been there with her household. In the house in Misenum, really small, she had no room for all her belongings or indeed for all her slaves; they slept under the olive trees for the most part, except the women she had to have with her. It belonged to an earlier part of her life, before she had bought the house in Rome. She valued it for its own sake, for the sea breeze that never failed in late afternoon and morning, and for the soldiers of the sea. Caesar's fleet had its principal base at Misenum.

On the second day after her arrival, recovering somewhat from her journey and her Roman agitations, Epicharis sent a slave with messages to several officers of her acquaintance, telling them that she had arrived. These officers of the sea troops had nothing to do with the management of the ships on which they sailed, of course—they were simply legionaries transferred to the boats—but somehow or other they had acquired, in the course of their experience on water, a different air, atmosphere, frame of mind and condition of soul from the soldiers who lived on the land. Epicharis had a weakness for the officers of the sea, partly because she had lived in Misenum for some years, and the sea soldiers were particularly happy to see a woman after their long voyages in the wide Mediterranean; but also because she relished in them some wild quality, not earthbound, which appealed to her own. They were away from their natural port as much as two or three weeks at a time, which brought them back to Misenum with a freshness of desire greatly in excess of anything known to Epicharis from land soldiers. They were not accustomed to giving her presents—indeed, she did not want them to do so—but their enthusiasm in the act of love made up for any amount of poverty. Indeed she had been known, from time to time, to give them presents herself: so well was she equipped with the world's goods by the benevolence of her Roman patrons. Thus she thought, in the hot season, to assuage her grief for the city.

But the boys did not come. The fleet was away, somewhere—Corsica, Marsilia—and no replies came to her notes. She was left with her own activities, the housekeeping, the books and the flowers, and with the news from Rome.

In every respect this news, coming every day with every possible distortion or exaggeration, infuriated her more and more. In the week after the great fire had died down, the week in which she arrived at Misenum, the Emperor and other authorities had ordered many great sacrifices and ceremonies at the surviving temples for the fate of Rome. The Emperor himself (whose house had also burned, and how? she asked herself, how?) participated in many of these grand and solemn ceremonies.

But the people of Rome said just what Epicharis said at Misenum: What is the good of this?

Belief in the ancient gods and their powers had declined to almost nothing, even among the people, whereas in the reigning classes it had long been a kind of deliberate mockery.

Will these sacrifices, these entrails of birds and these coils of incense, bring back my father, my mother, my son, my wife?

This is what the Roman people asked, and Epicharis, in Misenum, understood because her inquiry was the same.

She marched up and down her little garden and looked out to sea. Was it possible that these Roman tyrants, this Poppaea and this Nero, believed they could burn Rome and never pay a penalty?

Then, in the second week after the fire, two things happened: the news from Rome said that the incendiarism which had destroyed the city was now officially blamed upon the Jews, or rather upon one sect of the Jews; and the fleet came in from its wanderings.

The news from Rome was strange indeed. The Jews, an Oriental people with no reverence for the official gods, were not numerous, but in their humble way they had been useful artisans and merchants in Rome. Epicharis knew of them only that they worked, lived within themselves, had nothing to do with their surroundings, spoke very bad Latin and often no Greek, but took no part in the frequently violent outbursts of the mob. How could this inoffensive Oriental people be blamed for the burning of a vast city? There were not enough of them, really, to perform the physical act of setting it on fire.

She was puzzled by this news as much as she was pleased by the information (which she could indeed verify from her own garden on the hill) that Caesar's fleet was coming in to Misenum.

Another slave came in the afternoon with some more Roman news from the market place. He said that it was not all of the Jews, but one particular sect of them, called Chrestians, who had started the fire, and that these abominable Chrestians were now being interrogated by the authorities.

This gave Epicharis more bewilderment and even concern. She was a free woman of Greek origin and her father had been a Roman citizen, a centurion in the eleventh legion. In this situation, which had been improved by two marriages and gifts from generous friends, she was independent even if not rich, and she had never had any reason to know any Jews. They were, as she was informed, small merchants and moneylenders for the most part; there were not many of them; they were everywhere, chiefly in Alexandria, Athens, Rome, Ephesus, Marsilia, Carthage and other great cities; they had abandoned their native Jerusalem because it did not afford a living to their precise kind of talent. There were many such colonies of Orientals in Rome, and among them the Jews were not by any means the largest or the most conspicuous. (Hellenes, or Achaians, the most numerous of all foreigners, were not counted as Orientals: Epicharis herself was a Hellene by race and language: she was trying only to think of why the Jews should be blamed for burning Rome.)

Now the slave told her that "the authorities"—and she understood Caesar—wanted to put the blame for the catastrophe upon the special Jewish sect called Chrestian.

To this Epicharis had an instinctive rebellion. She had once known a Chrestian: the slave of a friend of hers, an old man who used to talk to her in Greek and give her remedies for sundry pains and aches. He was a learned man in his way, and his long, bony hands were good at rubbing away various pains and aches. It was a period when Epicharis had suffered from mysterious miseries in the knees, elbows and shoulders, attributed to an unusually foggy season. The old man, named Isocrates, was not a Greek from Achaia, but from some obscure province in Asia, possibly Judaea; Ephicharis could not remember. But she did remember with the utmost distinctness how the old fellow had talked and had soothed her pains. She had appreciated his voice as much as his long, hard fingers. She even remembered some of the things he had told her.

"The Chrestians?" she said to her own slave. "What do you mean by the Chrestians? They are mostly mild and simple people."

"I do not know, Lady," the slave said. "I am only repeating to you what I heard in the market. I was instructed to do so. I know nothing except what I heard."

His eyes were bent and his voice low. He was an Italian (not a Roman) and perhaps came from the Alps somewhere; she had bought him only a year before or less and really did not know him; he was a man of modest demeanor, medium stature and sturdy limbs, employed

chiefly in the garden, for marketing, and for other outside
tasks such as carrying messages. He was neither young nor
beautiful; young and beautiful slaves of either sex cost
three or four times as much as others and were completely
beyond Ephicharis's means, besides being unnecssary to
her.

"What does Caesar intend as a punishment for the Chrestians?" she asked in a hard but wondering voice.

"I do not know, Lady. I only repeat what I heard."

She had spoken to this man a number of times in the
garden, indeed she knew him, although not really well, and
she had never seen him behave in such a sheepish manner.
Her curiosity was aroused.

"Come, friend," she said in the coarsest Latin accent at
her command, "what's the matter with you? There is
something. You are disturbed, you are unhappy, you are
holding yourself within. What is it?"

His eyes opened and he looked at her: enormous brown
eyes, very dark brown, gazing at her very straight.

"Lady, I am a Chrestian," he said.

Startled, she rose from her chair.

"Go, man," she said, "and do not tell anybody else what
you have just said. And answer me this: Why have you
told me?"

"Because I must," he said.

If he had not been so submissive she could have called his
attitude even bold, because he stood very straight and his
deep brown eyes were fixed on hers.

"I will keep your secret," she said swiftly. "I have
known a Chrestian once, another slave. Go. Say nothing to
anybody about this. It is dangerous, very dangerous now.
If Caesar thinks the fire was set by the Chrestians he will

annihilate the sect. You are safe in my house. But you will not tell it to others."

"Lady," he said with the utmost tranquillity, "there is nothing secret about our sect. We meet from time to time and we all know each other. And we are born to die anyhow. That is what we think."

A terrible suspicion assailed her.

"Are there others in my household?" she asked. "How could I possibly know? Tell me the truth!"

"Yes, Lady, there are others," he said. His eyes were veiled again. The moment of boldness had passed.

She began to walk up and down on the stone flags of the middle garden.

"Do not tell me who they are," she said. "I never want to know who they are. I am sorry you told me that you were among these people. I knew one once, a Jew with a Greek name, the slave of a friend, who did me much good with his ministrations and talked to me a great deal. You believe in suffering as a means toward a better life, is that it?"

"It is too complicated, Lady," he said. "It is something like that. We are not afraid to die."

"But how can you believe in these Oriental superstitions?" she asked, suddenly angry with him. "It is a Jewish sect. You are not Jewish."

"Lady, I am Italian. I am from Cisalpine Gaul."

"What has that got to do with these Chrestians who—says Caesar—burned Rome?"

"Nothing, Lady. But our message is not only for Jews, even though our teacher was a Jew. Our message is for all people, everywhere."

"Go away from here at once, I tell you!" she said angrily. She was near to tears. "And do not tell anybody else about this, anybody else who does not already know. I forbid you. I will sell you, I will sell you on the auction block to a vulgar dealer, if you dare tell what you have told me. I do not want to have such people in my house."

He bowed deeply.

"I go, Lady," he said. "But we are not bad people. And certainly our people did not burn Rome."

She walked up and down nervously on her hilltop garden until another slave announced the arrival of two young sea soldiers known to her from previous summers. They asked permission to bring with them a superior officer. She told the slave to admit them and to fetch wine. It was near the sunset hour.

The two boys from the boats did not keep her attention long; she knew them both and had frolicked with them (separately, not together) during the preceding season; but they paled into immaturity before their superior officer, one Volusius Patroclus, a craggy, handsome man of about forty, who was as much bigger as he was older than his juniors. They, in their early twenties, were in awe of him, and might well have expected what happened, which was that Epicharis had no concern for them at all, but only for Patroclus. In their lively chatter, four-cornered as it was, the boys did most of the talking but Patroclus and Epicharis looked at each other and, when they spoke at all, spoke more deeply. There was nothing of any real consequence said, but she knew that he would return, which he did within an hour of their departure.

She could have made a virtuous pretext of household occupations, but she did not. It would have been absurd for a woman of the town like Epicharis to pretend to be virtuous; she was only discreet, another matter, and within her range she tried to be honest. Women of the very highest positions (the wife of the Emperor, indeed!) had exactly the same manners in this respect as she had. She was not a prostitute by any means and was not so registered under the law; she was the daughter of a Roman citizen and divorced wife of two Roman citizens; she had a small private fortune; she could do as she pleased, and those gifts which came her way from grateful partners of the bed had nothing to do with normal income or fiscal curiosity. She welcomed whom she chose to her house and her bed, and if they were perhaps a little more numerous than was the custom in previous times, it was not outside the habit of today.

Thus she did not make matters too difficult for Patroclus —indeed, he attracted her strongly. "Boys are nice," she told him, "but men are better." He laughed but said: "They are good boys," as if to defend his juniors, and she replied: "How well I know it—as they must have told you!" So everything was quite well understood between them before they had been alone for one minute together. It took very little longer to get them into bed, after the high Roman fashion, and when they had taken ample pleasure from their bodies they were disposed to a quieter form of intercourse. She particularly liked his voice, low indeed but not brutal, a mellow rumble which titivated her middle regions even when she had been amply gratified by stronger weapons. He was fascinated by her luscious body and her ease of manner, combined with the counterfeit aspect of a great lady: after all, Misenum was not Rome, and the sea soldiers did not meet suchlike often. After they had left her bedroom and resumed their clothing she sent for wine and fruit and they sat for a while in the atrium, open to the sea breeze.

They talked of the great fire, naturally. There was no other subject of general conversation at this moment anywhere, except in regions so remote as not yet to have heard the news. They had already talked of the great fire, in the late afternoon in the presence of the two boys, and they took it up again in the late evening by moonlight. Each had heard of horrors new to the other. Each had anxieties about friends or relatives. Each had heard unconfirmed stories of connected disasters, looting and raping and general outrage. Each was sparring about the central question of responsibility for the catastrophe, which both knew to be uppermost in every mind at this hour.

She broke it off.

"Have you heard of a Jewish religious sect called the Chrestians?" she asked him.

"I have heard of them and have seen a few, but I thought they were called Christians," he said. "In the eastern provinces, such as Asia, they exist."

"It could not make much difference what they are called," she said, "since Nero Claudius Caesar has decided that they are responsible for the burning of Rome."

"You are Greek, as I know by your name—or, that is, of Greek origin—and it is obviously some sort of Greek word, so tell me which ought it to be, Chrestian or Christian?"

"I cannot be sure," said she, rather nettled at being called Greek after two generations of Roman citizenship, "but I think it ought to be, correctly, that is, Chrestian. They are followers of some obscure agitator named Chrestos, as I have been told, who was executed in the reign of Tiberius Caesar. He was guilty of impiety toward the state as well as toward his native religion, that of the Jews."

"How can you know so much about these queer Jewish sects?" he inquired with genuine curiosity. It was, indeed, a surprising circumstance.

"I don't," she said. "It merely happened that a certain

friend of mine, one Claudia Livilla who was the widow of a centurion and owned very few slaves, had one old man who belonged to that sect. He was gifted with the rubbing of limbs, joints and bones. I was suffering from the bad air of Rome and Claudia Livilla sent her old slave to me every day for a while. He did me much good and while he was doing so he used to talk to me about his superstition."

"Abominable, no doubt," said Patroclus.

"No doubt," Epicharis agreed, "and yet it was very soothing. It seemed to go with the work he did with his hands. Half of the time I was asleep anyhow. But it was a benevolent thing, not a malevolent thing. In this respect my intellect rejects the hypothesis that such a sect of superstitious slaves could have burned Rome."

He sat back and looked into the high sky, past the moon. After a long silence he spoke again.

"Have you any other ideas?" he asked. "That is, if these Chrestians or Christians, whoever they may be, did not burn Rome, who did? Even I, an ignorant man of high birth, am aware that in the depths of the population nobody speaks of anything else. I am aware that everybody thinks the fire was deliberately planned, organized and exploited by somebody for some purpose. Have you any ideas on this subject? You seem to be, if I may say so, a woman of mind as well as body."

"This has been discovered before," she said tranquilly, and did not answer his question for a while. They drank their wine (Falernum it was, indeed!) and looked at the stars. The arches of the atrium were open in front and behind, and the little house was on the hill, so all the zephyrs of August were playing about them as in the poetry of their diverse ancestry. She leaned over to adjust the strap of her golden sandal and, having done so, consulted the moon again, and finally spoke.

"It is the Emperor, according to the people," she said deliberately.

"You have said that word, I did not say it," he said.

"Who else?" she asked.

"What do you know of the Emperor?" he asked, agitated and perhaps alarmed.

"Nothing," she said calmly. (It was a lie; everybody knew a great deal about the Emperor.) "All I know is that there is no other person or authority in this world who could order Rome to be burned from eighteen directions at once for one solid week. Who else has such power?"

He was silent for a long time.

"I must tell you," he said at last, "that I have been very badly treated by Caesar. He used me in one of his least avowable schemes, the murder of his mother. I did not realize that he truly intended to kill the old lady, but I obeyed my orders. It was that time when we went off to sea here, right here, from Misenum, and the ship fell apart. Nobody knew that the old lady was such a good swimmer. She got back under her own power."

"We all knew it, although not immediately," Epicharis said. "I was glad the woman escaped. When she was finally murdered, did you take part?"

"No," he said, "those were soldiers of the land, not soldiers of the sea."

"She was an evil but I am not at all sure that her son is not a greater evil," the woman said. It was in a garden at night and nobody was listening.

"Perhaps this is true," Patroclus said. "All I can tell you is that I never received any kind of reward, not even a word of thanks, from the Emperor for murdering his mother."

"This seems a legitimate grievance," Epicharis said ironically, suffering from the reaction which follows sexual intercourse. At this moment the sea soldier did not even seem to her moderately intelligent, although still handsome. "And yet I understood you to say that you had not, in point of fact, murdered the late Agrippina?"

"I did not," said Patroclus. "I commanded the ship in which she was supposed to die. I was supposed to die too, perhaps. So were we all. It parted in the middle, according to some clever design of the Emperor's engineers. It was supposed to sink at once with all on board, except that we, the sea soldiers, were provided with small boats as always. I had no instructions as to what to do with the Empress. As the whole world knows, she swam ashore, the dirty old bitch. These events took place two years ago and the Emperor has not yet rewarded me."

"How very remiss of him!" Epicharis said. "I find that he has other faults besides his ingratitude to you. I believe it is not at all impossible that Rome was burned at his order and under his plan. I believe that these utterly harmless Jews, Chrestians or Christians or whatever they may be called, may be exterminated for a crime they did not commit, but which, instead, Caesar himself committed, and for which he dare not take the blame before the people of Rome and their posterity."

"Lady," said the craggy commander with some reverence, "I think you have more brains than I have."

"It is possible," Epicharis said briskly. "It is also possible that you should go home. It is almost midnight, which is very late for Misenum."

"I will go, lovely Lady, if I may come back," he said,

drawing himself to his oceanic height. She perceived that he was by now just a tiny bit drunk, as a result of much wine following a species of sexual exhaustion. She was suddenly filled with a disgust for all men, although she could never have lived a single day without them.

"Go, noble Roman," she said, "and perhaps tomorrow I may tell you some way in which you can regain your manhood."

"What?" said he, aghast at words he could scarcely hear.

"The ingratitude of Caesar," she said, crushed against his half-metallic breast, "for the unsuccessful murder of his impossible mother."

"I don't know what you say," he murmured in her ear, "but you are what you are, and I want to come again."

"You shall come," she said rapturously, "and I shall tell you how to regain your manhood."

When she returned to her quarters, after she was sure that the slaves had shown him out and down the steps and into the cobbled street, she thought for a moment. A fool, of course: the man was a fool. But such as these were the best instruments because they knew nothing, understood nothing, foresaw nothing. Let him be a fool. She would use him to free the city. And with the city there was the state, and with the state there was the Empire, and the Empire was the world.

She went to bed in a state of consciousness which, before it yielded to darkness, was half dream and half hope.

BY THE TIME Epicharis had taught Patroclus to "regain his manhood," which took her about ten days, he knew very nearly as much as she did about the conspiracy in which she wished to enlist his services.

This happened bit by bit, not as an articulated revelation, and never completely. Indeed sometimes the woman would tell him one detail on Monday and deny it on Tuesday. Her supreme object was to get him to undertake the actual murder of Caesar, which she felt should be accomplished at sea for the sake of the greater security of the conspiring patriots. She had always rebelled against the idea of killing the tyrant in the midst of Rome, where any whim on the part of his plebeian admirers might overwhelm the conspirators and bring an unknown but fatal result. Out at sea, on a ship commanded by Patroclus, there could be no sudden insanity of the city mob—the deed would be cold by the time it became known in the city. She felt sure that an emperor already dead for perhaps two days would not arouse the passion of the Romans as one killed before their eyes—one whom they had long, obstinately and unreasonably loved, even though the dark rumors of a different emotion had now begun to undermine him. Thus she strove in devious ways, first with one approach and then with another, to enlist Patroclus, and it was clear that she had no stronger argument in her persuasive enterprise than the numbers and names of the noble Romans already pledged to the deed. She did not name them all, by any means, and sometimes after she had allowed a name to slip out she afterwards told him she had been wrong—that he had misunderstood; that she had not said thus and so, but quite otherwise. She did not much confuse him. Before her own subtleties he was stupid indeed, but in a straightforward matter of life and death he knew his way. Quite early he understood that she wanted to use him as a direct instrument—not perhaps his own hand, but the ship he commanded—in the murder of Nero Claudius Caesar. That fact stood out from all the floods of unrelated detail in which she often plunged her discourse.

Nor was he, at first, completely deaf to her persuasions. His grievance against Caesar was real. For Nero he had undertaken a great crime, at enormous risk, and had never received the slightest recompense or even acknowledgment. The crime now proposed to him—at long last, after much irrelevant advancing and retreating, days of the most complicated praeludium—was not essentially worse than the other: indeed it had some claim to moral superiority, in that tyrannicide had often been esteemed and matricide always abhorred. But where the hard-fisted Patroclus grew doubtful was upon the chances of success and the results of failure. He could not make out what guaranties Epicharis had, if any, on the treatment to be given the instrument of such a deed; he was not altogether sure that she had the authority to make any agreement, or even to utter the suggestions that she did make. He could not obtain from her any fixed or sure list of the leading figures in the conspiracy; what names she did divulge, reluctantly and by way of argument, did not seem to stand in the front rank of the Roman nobles; and even these she was likely to retract in the next conversation. He felt at times that he had fallen into a purely feminine imaginary drama, a fabric of solitary dreaming crossed perhaps (as he seemed to discern) with some vengeful hatred toward Poppaea. If this were all, if this were, in fact, the sum and substance of his dalliance, he had no worries—she was a luscious woman and his pleasure with her was great, even if she did talk a weird and sanguinary nonsense between times.

Yet he could not, for more than a few moments at a time, convince himself that Epicharis's incessant plotting and planning was mere wish-drama or a form of entertainment. The woman was too intense. Sometimes she trembled with the sheer violence of her own feeling. Vague, contradictory, incomprehensible as were some of the gobbets of information she disgorged, there was no real doubt in his mind that there *was* information—it was too circumstantial to be the product of an idle daydream. These men, many of whom he did not even know by name, had a real existence: he had easily verified it by casual inquiry. Whether they were engaged in as desperate an undertaking as she made out—whether they even knew each other—he could not determine unaided, since he knew none of them, and it seemed to him that the only course open, if he wished to find out how much of her story was true, would be to go to Rome and inquire point-blank from one or two of the persons she had named.

At the first hint of any such project she had broken into a storm of protest, accusations and tears. He wished to ruin her with her only friends; he wanted to make life in Rome impossible for her in future; he would subject her to the odium of having betrayed secrets and endangered her nearest and dearest. He had no pity, no comprehension, no love; she who had trusted him with her life was to be betrayed for nothing, merely because he could not take her word for the simplest facts. And he had promised nothing; he was not with her; he did not love her; he would throw away her life and happiness without a thought, out of sheer curiosity, having promised nothing whatsoever in return.

It was, although neither had put it into words before, the plain truth that he had promised nothing. He had listened, he had asked questions, he had even discussed possibilities, but he had promised nothing. So far as her actual project was concerned, Epicharis had advanced no further with him since the idea dawned on her during their first night together. She had played heavily on the theme of love—that she was in love with him and had been from the first moment—and perhaps he believed her in this, a matter easier to accept than conspiracy. But never had he given his word to do as she wished.

On that evening she succeeded in dissuading him from the threatened visit to Rome, which could well have ruined her plan. (What could Lucan or Lateranus, Sulpicius or

Subrius or any of the others, say to a rude, broad question? What, indeed?) She was ready to present her instrument to the conspirators once she was sure of the instrument. So far, nothing had encouraged her to such assurance, and she dreaded the catastrophe of a premature revelation. For her, at any rate, it could be nothing less than catastrophe, robbing her in one moment of all the best, richest and most powerful of her friends, those who had made life so agreeable in recent years and whose protection had come to seem essential. She had not a shred of claim upon them once it became known that she had trifled with their secrets. Their wrath would be terrible, and it would be just. She had been rash to confide anything at all to this blundering fool, who was capable of thinking he could walk up to a noble Roman in the midst of the Forum and ask point-blank: "Is it true that you are conspiring against the life of the Fifth Casear?" Patroclus had not said just how he meant to proceed, but he had said he would "inquire" from some of the associates, and how else could one inquire in such a matter?

Vexed and frightened, it was long before Epicharis slept that night.

In the morning, pale and tired and low in spirit, she was sitting in the garden on the hill when a note was brought to her: Patroclus was under orders, had proceeded out to sea at dawn, would call upon her at the moment of his return, perhaps in two or three weeks.

Her relief was so tremendous that she felt as if he had reprieved her from a death sentence, as perhaps (without knowing it) he had. She rose like a new woman to the cares of her household and her own beauty, which had seemed so dreary only a few moments ago; she made up her mind to ask some young officers for wine in the evening; she vowed that she would not say one word about public affairs, or the great fire, or Nero Claudius Caesar; if others spoke of such things she would be mute; until Patroclus returned and reverted to the subject she would exclude it, so far as possible, even from her mind. She had the feeling that it had been a mistake from the beginning to suppose that Patroclus could be tamed to her purpose. She knew men well, or had long supposed so, and yet in this case she had made an error of almost fatal gravity.

She was able to keep her vow of silence on public matters with immense difficulty, not because older subjects came up during the day or at the evening gathering with the young officers, but because a new source of horror and loathing was provided by the news from Rome. A wholesale torture of the Jewish-Chrestian sect had begun on the greatest scale which their somewhat limited numbers allowed. The first news was brought to Epicharis by her own Italian slave whom she already knew, by his own confession, to be a member of this sect. He looked at her, wide-eyed and a little pale, and told her what he had heard in the market place that morning.

"They are used as human torches in the imperial gardens," he said, "or they were so used last night. They were drenched with oil and then set afire. The people of Rome were invited to the Palatine to see the spectacle."

She moaned with disgust. There were times when her detestation of the Emperor and all his doings made her physically sick.

"Yesterday they were devoured by wild dogs," the slave said. "Tomorrow they may be given to the lions."

"I cannot endure hearing about it," she said. "Please do not tell me any more. Above all, be silent about your own relation to these matters. I know you set no fires in Rome.

You were with me the whole time outside the city, on the Pincian Hill. I know it. So be quiet. Do not attract attention to this house. And I cannot stand hearing of any more horrors."

"Lady, you have always wanted to know the reports and rumors from the market place," the slave said mildly. "It has been my order."

"But not this," she said in distraction. "Not this, not this! I cannot endure it. It is so senseless, needless, false, cruel— Oh, please do not tell me any more, tomorrow or any other day!"

It was all very well to shut the slave's mouth and try to forget what he had said, but it was a different matter with the three young maritime officers who came to call and drink wine at sunset.

They were handsome, high-spirited boys whom she had known for a previous summer or two. None of them served under Patroclus, of course, or they would have been far at sea by now. They had actually only the minimal interest in public affairs, government, or the Empire, and yet it was beyond their capacity to refrain from discussing that which everybody else discussed at the same moment. Just now this one subject of discussion, which was undoubtedly uniform not only in Misenum but for miles in all directions, was the torture, punishment and execution of the Chrestian Jews.

"I don't care what they've done," one boy declared hotly. "They are human beings the same as everybody else. If they have committed crimes they should be punished. If they set fire to some houses in Rome they should be put to death. I would have no mercy on them. But I would not convert them into living torches for the amusement of the vulgar mob."

"There is a certain justice in making torches out of them," another young man put in. "That is, if they are guilty of setting torches to the city. This city which has lasted so many long centuries—to be ended by the foul superstition of some Orientals! It is too much for me to bear with philosophic calm, I may say. More wine, dear Lady. I will send you some tomorrow."

Epicharis knew perfectly well that none of these young men would ever send her wine or other gifts, but she poured his goblet full. She did not trust herself to speak but she took some strange, sour pleasure in hearing them talk.

"I have never seen or heard the slightest proof that they did set fire to the city," the third boy said slowly. "For three or four weeks it was quite another story that we heard. Is it not possible—I don't know—that this is made up to take the place of the other story?"

"The other story?" the first boy asked with a painful, sneering laugh. "The other story?"

"Of course. We all know it. We are safe here. The story that was believed, up to now, is that the Emperor himself gave the orders."

"Who is to know?" the first boy asked. "I don't say the Jews did not do it. I know nothing about them, but I have heard that they hate the human race. All I have said is that *they* are human beings and not to be treated as torches for the pleasure of the lowest mob."

"It is not the Jews, anyhow," said the thoughtful third in the trio. "It is one of their sects. I forget the name. All members of this particular sect are to be executed. The Jews in general are not, up to this moment, involved in the matter."

"I don't care," the first boy said. "They're all Orientals

and I cannot tell them apart. But I don't want them to be put to death in these strange and barbarous ways. To me the idea of human beings as torches is in itself alien to Rome, to Romanism and to civilization. It sounds like the tortures we hear about from Asia and beyond—in fact, it is Oriental, like the persons being punished."

"It is hard to find anybody in the streets of Rome today who is not Oriental," the dissident second boy put in. "I could not weep if they were all destroyed. They have taken over the city as it is. If these foreigners are guilty I have no sympathy for them, no matter how horrible the punishment."

"Please!" Epicharis said. "Can we not talk of something else? This is—well, not pleasant on a beautiful evening."

"It is indeed a beautiful evening," the first boy said after a brief and startled stare at her. "I did not realize that you were so tender-hearted, dear Epicharis. Of course we must speak of something else. It is only difficult because the one subject of conversation everywhere in Italy today is this public torture, this public sacrifice. Forgive me, dear friend."

"There is nothing to forgive," she said a little wildly, pushing her hair back from her brow. "I know nothing of these things. But there have been so many horrors, so many cruelties—sometimes I think I cannot bear any more. This one comes at the end of a long, long . . ." Her voice died away and she rose to pour wine. "Let us drink," she said, "and talk of pleasanter things."

This was possible on that one night, although with difficulty. It proved impossible during the next few weeks because nobody could be induced to abandon the subject of the wholesale destruction of this Eastern sect. Every detail was rehearsed a thousand times by slaves, neighbors and guests, until Epicharis felt that she did not wish to speak again to any human creature. Worst of all was the gloating delight which came into many eyes and voices as they retailed the latest inventions of horror, the newest refinements of torture, wreaked by Caesar upon his chosen victims. The facts alone were horrible, but for others at a distance, immune from the insanity of blood, to recite such facts with sensuous gratification—this, to Epicharis, was the ultimate disgust. She came in the course of about three weeks to a kind of self-imprisonment, inviting nobody to her house and never going out, forbidding her slaves to speak to her and burying herself, as much as her determination could effect it, in books long-tried and often read, the poets and philosophers of her own race.

She was thus found, enclosed as in a chrysalis, when Patroclus returned from his tour of duty at sea.

It was her duty to receive him with joy, and she could only hope that the terror at the center of her being escaped his notice. They had a long, tender and amorous evening and not a word was spoken of that which filled her with dread. Only as he was about to go away, very late at night or early in the morning, did he say some words which congealed her blood for a moment.

"Your plans for the great one," he said carelessly, "are they the same as ever?"

"Oh, don't speak of them!" she said hastily. "We can talk another time. It is late now. So much has happened, dear one, that I do not think of all those things we discussed weeks ago. Let it go. Forget it for the moment. We can talk tomorrow."

But on the morrow he had not forgotten and indeed he did begin to talk, in the form she found least welcome: he was now asking questions almost without end. She tried in vain to divert him. He would come back again and again to the conspiracy, inquiring after names and dates, persons and places, plans and hopes. He was most concerned with pinning down, so far as he could, the actual names and public ranks of the associates. Obviously during his long weeks at sea (it had been less than three, but now in retrospect they seemed many, a long interval of peace) he had been thinking deeply over everything she had ever told him. She spent her entire time avoiding the answers to his questions, mystifying him when possible, deluding or overwhelming him with love: anything to keep him away from the truth which now, too late, seemed to her a devouring monster.

Then there came a day when he was not in Misenum and not at sea either. His ship was there (she could see it from her garden) but he did not come or send messages, and he did not reply to a message she wrote to him late in the afternoon. The slave who took it returned to tell her that the captain was not in Misenum. She felt cold fingers at her throat.

"Where do they think he has gone?" she asked with as much indifference as she could pretend.

"They do not know, Lady," the slave said. "Perhaps to Rome."

Epicharis shuddered and grew silent for a long time, cold in the afternoon sunlight. There seemed to her nothing to do but wait. If any of her friends, her Roman friends, had been at hand—but no matter, they were not; and moreover she could not think of how to tell them what had now befallen her, the ghastly mistake she had made, the fatal error in judgment, the desire to help gone woefully wrong. Not once had she wished anything but good, anything but success, to her friends. And yet she knew, somehow, even before there was any proof of it, that she had not only failed them dismally, but had put them into mortal danger. It was meddling, it was interference in matters of which she knew next to nothing, it was female hubris at its worst: her pride had convinced her that she knew better than her friends. And she had been most solemnly warned against it—by Lucan chiefly, or by Lucan among others: he had begged her to do nothing whatsoever, particularly at Misenum, particularly with her friends of the fleet. She could see his angular young face, not handsome but to her powerfully attractive, as he implored her to forget all such ideas. And then—and then what had she done?

On the third day after the disappearance of Patroclus, at a time when Epicharis felt that she could not endure any more waiting without a loss of sanity, the legionaries came. There were four of them, with a centurion to command them, and they said she must pack and return to her house in Rome under their escort. The centurion was a handsome young officer who may have seen and coveted Epicharis before at a distance, perhaps in a theater or in the streets: he was most courteous and even deferential to her, and his dark eyes betrayed his admiration. She was to be given a few hours—the fewest needed—to pack her belongings and return to her house in Rome.

Calmly, without manufacturing obstacles or delays, she put her slaves to the task, which she herself supervised. It was neither long nor difficult. Without the one who had disappeared in the fire (or rather, she thought, run away) and the one who had been left to guard the house in Rome, she had only five here, two of them women, but they were enough to bale up everything she had brought with her from the city. In a litter provided by the public authorities, with relays of road slaves to carry it, she would make a return journey no less dignified and comfortable than that which had been arranged for her by the consul-elect on coming hither. There was one great difference, a difference as great as the world: she had no idea of what awaited her at the end of this journey.

THE VENGEANCE OF CAESAR was the last thing Patroclus desired or foresaw in his journey to Rome. He was, in the
first place, an extremely stupid man. Those ideas he had
and was capable of retaining for any space of time were
clear enough, but few and insusceptible of modification. At
the present moment, in the balance of personal advantage,
he thought it more reasonable to tell Caesar what he knew
or suspected than to keep a highly uncertain secret which
in itself offered him no advantage. Caesar already owed him
gratitude. Now it would be a multiplication of gratitude,
or so he assumed, and he would glean a great harvest from

the information which, unclear and contradictory although it might seem, he had to offer to the Master of the World.

There were many things he forgot or had never known. He did not realize that it would take him two entire days to penetrate to the private attention of Tigellinus, copraefect of the praetorians, although his message had declared it a matter of life or death. He had never expected to be greeted with suspicion or subjected to the most humiliating interrogations. He did not know that his slightest word would be submitted to the judgment of experts. He was unaware of the fact that his every deed or word in the maritime service of the Empire was on record in Rome and had to be perused and weighed by the knowers on high. Least of all did he realize that his part in the unsuccessful shipwreck of the Emperor's mother two years before—a duty which had to him become a grievance because unrecompensed—was in fact the gravest doubt upon his record, and the only one which those in highest places remembered.

Nero himself knew nothing else of the man.

"Patroclus?" he said. "Volusius Patroclus? Ah, yes, ah, yes, the commander of the ship . . ."

He would say no more on that subject but everybody in his close surroundings understood a reference to Agrippina —that is, to the mother whom he could never bear to mention since her murder. What made it even more intolerable was that Patroclus was combined in Nero's mind with the *unsuccessful* matricide, the elaborate plot about the ship which was to part in the middle, and did, but was defeated by the old lady's powerful swimming. This had been one of the greatest disappointments in the life of the Fifth Caesar and he was inclined to blame it principally upon the commander Patroclus, who ought somehow to have made the plot work even though the imperial lady was indomitable.

It was therefore Nero's instantaneous command, on hearing of the information brought by Patroclus, to degrade the man of all rank or rights and submit him to the torture.

"It is possible, Lord," Tigellinus told him, "that the fellow is telling the truth or some part of the truth. He is an ox, a perfect ox, of stupidity and ignorance. He professes to get all his information from a certain Roman lady of Greek origin by the name of Epicharis, now in Misenum."

"I have heard of this lady," the Emperor said. Indeed he had, and with avid interest, since he loved to peruse the daily reports of the informers (the "delators") who told what everybody had done in the preceding twenty-four hours. "It would seem to me that among my closest friends are some who have enjoyed the intimacy of this lady. I have owned a certain curiosity about her myself, since she has the art to seduce both young and old. She has had Lucan for a year or more, and she has the consul-elect Lateranus. I can see no element of common passion which could attract her to both."

"Lord, and permit me to say, as your deified father did, Lord and God!"

Nero laughed. Any reference to his deified father (that is, to his adoptive father Claudius, formally deified after death) always made him laugh, and especially if it concerned the combination of "Lord and God" (*dominus et deus*) which Claudius was the first of the Romans to authorize for himself.

"Bring the lady to Rome, of course," the Emperor said negligently. "Treat her kindly. She is no doubt either totally innocent of any thought in public matters, or is a chatterer with no knowledge. I hear that she is very good in bed and some day I may try her myself. Any woman who can keep that sour, long-nosed Lucan, with his puny penis, must be an adept at her craft. Bring her here and talk to her. I might even talk to her myself. The chances are that she knows nothing of all this nonsense. The fellow Patroclus is to blame, believe me—he betrayed me once and he can do it again."

So Patroclus, the stupid man, vanished into suffering and sorrow and, after weeks of it, into death. Never did he know how his calculations had been erroneous.

Epicharis had not the slightest difficulty. All she had to do was to deny all knowledge of the conspiracy which Patroclus had denounced. She did not know the names he had mentioned, except those which were in the public knowledge or those which (like Lucan, Lateranus and a few others) she knew to be on the police records as visitors to her house. She was herself quite innocent of thought. She had never considered the fate of the Roman Empire as being within her concern. She loved poetry, plays, music, flowers and men. Of these, it was her considered judgment that poetry came first, and in her extremely brief interview with the Emperor (Tigellinus brought her in for a little less than ten minutes) it was this which did her most good.

"Well, now, if you speak from the heart," the Emperor said, "I am inclined to consider you absolved of all guilt. The love of poetry washes everything else away. At the same time I must ask you, if you can endure the question, whether you have read any of my own poetry?"

Epicharis had.

Thus would all things have remained—and Patroclus tortured to death—if there had not arisen some other circumstances which shocked the dwellers on the Palatine.

A Senator named Flavius Scaevinus, quite unknown to the lady Epicharis, had undertaken the task of killing Nero Claudius Caesar.

He had willingly assumed the duty or honor, among all the other conspirators, because he had a dagger from the Temple of Fortune which in his own opinion could not fail to do its act of fate. The conspirators in general had been quite unmoved by the arrest of Patroclus and Epicharis, since these obscure persons were unknown to most of them, but they had at least become aware of it and of the rumor that it involved Romans of high rank. There was unease in the great houses. Many landed proprietors journeyed to their country estates in Campania, or on the Adriatic, or to the north, without any really seasonable excuse for doing so, especially after it became known that Flavius Scaevinus was being questioned in regard to the same matters.

Scaevinus had a favored slave named Milichus, whom he had set free some time before, and in whom his confidence was almost without limit. It was to Milichus that he gave the dagger from the Temple of Fortune with instructions to sharpen the point and edge to their keenest. Milichus was also to prepare bandages and ligatures for wounds. Perhaps his information ran wider and deeper than this, since his opportunities in the house were innumerable; he might have overheard conversations among the conspirators for a year or more. And on the last night before the plot was to come to a head, Scaevinus made his will, set his favored slaves free, distributed gifts of money and sat down to a grand banquet in a state of deep, thoughtful depression.

What had been decided—and because of the arrest of

Patroclus it was a little earlier than might have been—was to murder Nero at the circus games in honor of Ceres, when he would be far more accessible than in his own new palace, the House of Gold. The consul-elect Lateranus, who was an enormous man, would throw himself at Caesar's knees and, grasping them, would thus upset the Emperor and hold him to the ground. At this point Scaevinus would strike the first blow, immediately followed by all the military men in attendance or otherwise to be found on the spot—officers of the praetorian guard or the legions who, like the knights Subrius and Sulpicius, had formed part of the conspiracy from the beginning. Caius Piso would be waiting in the sanctuary of Ceres until summoned forth by Faenius Rufus to be proclaimed emperor then and there.

That was how it was to go.

In the event, it was altogether otherwise, since Milichus, at dawn on the festival of Ceres, went to the Palatine Hill and after repeated attempts to get in, and repeated warnings of the grave nature of his errand, was conducted to the presence of the rich freedman Epaphroditus (the owner of the Stoic slave Epictetus) who, after hearing the gist of the matter, took him at once to Nero. The Emperor got out of his luxurious bed to hear one of the most horrifying stories that had come his way since childhood: to him, who believed in and treasured popularity beyond any other gift, the idea that so many people of all ranks desired and plotted his death was a true shock. The freedman Milichus bade him question Scaevinus himself if there remained any doubt.

There followed the crumbling of the defenses which a year and a half had not sufficed to build solidly around the conspiracy. Scaevinus boldly denied everything and attacked his freedman Milichus with scorn, but the latter remembered in time that Antonius Natalis had been the last to have a long, secret talk with Scaevinus and said so. At this Natalis also was arrested, and he and Scaevinus, questioned separately about their conversation of the previous evening, gave such widely differing answers that they were consigned to the torture. Before it could begin both had yielded—first Natalis, then Scaevinus—giving names and details lavishly.

Nero, stung into rapid action by the shock of these revelations, took charge of the arrests and tortures for the next two or three days himself, besides bringing in the legions (filled with barbarians by now) from outlying regions to garrison and patrol the city. His own guard was heavily augmented and he remained in the House of Gold, while the festival of Ceres went forward without him and without most of the notables of Rome.

He bethought himself of the woman Epicharis, who was still being held, although he had been inclined to believe her denials. Now he ordered her, too, to be put to the torture, which after a whole day elicited nothing from her but further denials. She knew nothing of any conspiracy and did not recognize most of the names mentioned to her. On the second day of her torture, although her body was quite broken, she had told nothing, and was being carried to the rack again when she contrived by some ingenious means to get a piece of her clothing tightened round her neck enough to bring about, in her weakened condition, a strangulation which was not noticed until it was complete.

The noble Romans whom she had protected by her torture and death were not so steadfast. Some lasted longer than others. The threat of torture had been enough for Scaevinus and Natalis; its reality, whether for an hour or for a day or more, proved to be enough for most of their friends. There were among them persons who did not affront the torture at all, but eagerly accepted the illusory rewards offered for information; these, too, found death to be the end of it.

Caius Calpurnius Piso might have taken a last desperate chance on the day of the festival, before much had yet been revealed, by appealing to the people and the legions against the tyrant; the sworn conspirators, having nothing to lose, would join him, and perhaps a movement of revolt could thus be started; it was at least better than awaiting death at home. So his friends argued. He preferred to wait in his own house until the soldiers came, and then, with their permission, to open his veins and die.

Day after day they were arrested in their throngs, the knights and nobles, soldiers and praetorians, hundreds upon hundreds of them every day, until it seemed that there would be no end to the destruction and that there would be few left to conduct the business of the state or the discipline of the armed forces. A great many false accusations must certainly have been made, as always when terror and violence reign; private vengeance cannot fail to take advantage of public distress. The number of those truly involved in the so-called conspiracy of Piso, the conspiracy which centered around Piso, could never be known under such circumstances. It was a large number, certainly, but those who died for it were even more numerous, and a certain number of others, never to be determined, escaped by negligence or accident from the net of Caesar's revenge.

Without pretending a guilty knowledge of the plot, which would have been difficult even for her to justify, Poppaea took an active part in the punishment of the accused, whether they were guilty or innocent. The whole apparatus of torture fascinated her and she had many private grudges to pacify. If the Emperor's resolute cruelty failed for even a moment—if he hesitated over the execution of a childhood friend, for instance—he had only to seek the company of Poppaea and Tigellinus to be rendered more ferocious than before. Poppaea actually enjoyed being present, although concealed, at the torture of those who had for any reason offended her in the past. Their cries of agony were a pleasure to her. To add to her happiness at this period she had become pregnant again, and the joys of future empire were superimposed upon the powers of the present.

There were delays just as curious as the most hurried executions. The consul-elect Lateranus, for example, whose rank should have given him the alternative of suicide, was put to death in a place for the execution of slaves, with no time to make a will or say good-bye to his children, and his executioner (or more precisely butcher) was a tribune who had been in the conspiracy. Several of the plotters, holding rank in the guards or the legions, distinguished themselves by their zeal in punishing their less lucky friends. Even Faenius Rufus, who enjoyed the hatred of both Poppaea and Tigellinus, remained by some accident immune for several weeks, either because no prisoner had remembered to denounce him, or because such denunciation had not been believed. Indeed it would have been difficult to believe offhand, without some shadow of proof, that the co-commander of the Emperor's own bodyguard could be guilty. So Faenius, for his own safety, became one of the most enthusiastic persecutors of the accused, many of whom were his close friends. His knowledge of Rome and of the imperial justice was unsurpassed, and yet he seems to have believed that by such tactics he might save himself from the end which Tigellinus had long intended for him.

Lucan, for whom Nero was willing to spare the torture at first, was obstinate in his denials of every name and every detail for a long time. Some of his friends, Senecio and Quintianus for instance, were equally determined. They were among the first to be arrested and among the last to yield information. By the time they did, it was of no use, but the blackness of the story would be incomplete without saving that they, too, gave the names of their best friends.

On the day when the plot was betrayed—that is, on the festival of Ceres in the late autumn—Lucan was informed very early, by friends on the Palatine, what had happened. His uncle Seneca was at this time in Campania at another villa; the one in the Sabine Hills was too cold, at this season, for his aged bones, and he sought the sun. Lucan knew at once, when he was told that both Scaevinus and Natalis were under arrest, that there would be no uprising, and perhaps no festival of Ceres, on that day. As a last act of piety before he, too, should be arrested, he thought it his duty to warn his uncle. Nothing could avert fate but there was some strength in being prepared for it. He took horse at once (it was still early morning) and rode for the south.

At Seneca's villa he was received in mid-afternoon with some caution. Paulina had no great admiration for her husband's nephew, whose conduct she thought rash; his poetry was dangerously republican in her eyes; his friends were irreverent and debauched. She told him that his uncle was resting and should not be disturbed. He could rest himself, after his long ride, and refresh himself with food and wine and the bath, and talk to his uncle toward sunset. As he had no choice in the matter, Lucan obeyed, although his imagination was busy constructing a thousand febrile versions of what might be going on in Rome. He would have to stay the night in any case and return by early morning, so an hour or two more could make no difference.

When he was summoned to his uncle's presence it was on another sunny terrace in late afternoon, much sunnier and warmer than the terrace at the Sabine villa. Here Seneca sat in a big armchair, looking even thinner and paler than he had in July, four months earlier. He was wasting away, Lucan thought, through sheer refusal to eat anything but roots and herbs, fruits and nuts. Whether these austerities were due to the fear of poison or to the philosopher's contempt for the body none could say: by now the two had become mixed. The old man raised his head and looked steadily at his nephew.

"Lucanus," he said, "nothing good brings you here so unexpectedly. What has happened?"

"There was a conspiracy against Caesar," Lucan said bluntly. "You knew. You must have known even though you refused to listen. I don't know how much you knew— enough to realize that many are involved, and also that I am among them."

"They attempted to bring me into it but I have always refused," the old man said. "That is, if I know what you mean, and I believe I do."

"Well, it has been discovered. This morning there were two men arrested, Scaevinus and Natalis, and before sunset there must be many more arrested, because those two men will have talked. I will return to Rome tomorrow morning, as early as possible, so that I may be arrested also if I am named along with all the others."

"Why have you traveled so far to tell me this?" Seneca asked. "I have always known that this harebrained conspiracy, of which I knew little, would be betrayed or would fail in some manner. The services at Caesar's disposal are too many and too great. Among your very conspirators there may have been some who were his agents."

"I think not," said Lucan. "I think the secret has been well kept until now. The deed—the climax—was to have been today, and it is only today, very early in the morning, that the first arrests took place."

"It was bound to be so," Seneca said with remarkable tranquillity.

"I have come only to warn you," Lucan said. "Many of these men are convinced that you were with us. Some of them actually hoped that you would take the Empire rather than Caius Piso, who was our leader. You are in danger because you may have been named by many of the suspected or arrested men. I speak plainly."

"I thank you," Seneca said calmly. "I am ready for whatever may come. I have been ready for at least two years. I do not expect anything except death. I had nothing to do with this conspiracy—indeed I have resisted every attempt made to involve me, and there were several—but that makes no difference. Caesar will be happy to remove me from this earth. I am not at all reluctant to go. It will be known in the future that I was not guilty of conspiring to murder the Emperor or of thinking, even thinking, of the power of the Empire in these circumstances. That is the principal thing. I am guiltless but quite ready to be punished just the same."

"There is nothing you or anybody can do," Lucan said broodingly. "I only came to warn you. I only came so that you could be ready."

) 2 3 0 (

"I am already ready and have been for a long time," the old man said. "As a matter of fact, I shall go to Rome soon, within two or three days, or rather to my villa on the Via Nomentana. It is very near Rome. It will be better for me to await whatever comes there. It is more convenient for everybody. They will not have so far to travel when they come."

Lucan sat silent for a space of time while the old man stared out at the Tyrrhenian Sea, visible afar in the sunset. Finally the young poet spoke.

"I was going to spend the night and return to Rome early in the morning," he said. "Perhaps it would be best to get a start now. I am rested and refreshed, I have bathed and had food and wine."

"It would be very fatiguing to go now," Seneca said. "You must be tired, and to return to Rome would be a killing journey."

"I should not like it to be said that I ran away," Lucan pointed out, "or that I took refuge of any kind with you. It would only make your own case worse."

"Nothing can do that," the old man said indifferently, "but of course you must do as you like. If you think you can ride so many more hours—it seems to me impossible."

"I can get a long start," Lucan said. "Then, when I am really worn out, I can stop and rest for a few hours, and anyhow be at my own house on the Caelian Hill in the morning. If I sleep the night here I can only be at home by tomorrow afternoon."

"You must do as you like," Seneca said. "It was good of you to come here to warn me, even though it was not necessary. I am ready."

Lucan stood and saluted. He was curiously moved, more than he could have believed to be within his own nature, at this parting from a relative who had, for good or ill, over-shadowed his life.

"Brother of my father, farewell," he said.

"Lucanus, farewell," the old man replied, turning his quiet gaze on his nephew. "Farewell," he repeated, as if to strengthen the knowledge between them that they would not meet again.

XV

WHEN THE OLD MAN ARRIVED at his villa Nomentana, four miles from Rome, it was five days later and events had taken place of which he had no knowledge. His ears were obsessed by the crying of women. He had heard it first a few miles below Rome, in some villages which were not far from the city and had their own temples. It sounded like the funebrious exercises of the women bereaved, as they were forever being bereaved, and he thought nothing of it beyond the acknowledgment of ever-present death.

Seneca was now approaching seventy and could easily

have been ten years older because of the austerities he prac-
ticed, if not because of the burden of his thought. He was
gaunt, gray, sad. When he was required to walk he did so
with the aid of a long staff. He was shaved and close-
cropped on the head, as was customary in this time, but if
he had allowed his hair and beard to grow he might have
been an immensely venerable apparition by now. His eyes,
ever the most active part of his physiognomy, were sharper
and bluer than ever before, sustaining an interrogation, an
assessment and a final judgment which his tongue had long
since given up as useless.

Most of his personal and household slaves had preceded
him from Campania to the villa on the Via Nomentana. He
and Paulina had progressed by easy stages, resting at
night or even by day if it seemed necessary. From the Via
Appia to the Via Nomentana, by means of one of those
myriad crossroads which sustained the system of great
highways, his party and escort succeeded in avoiding the
city altogether, although in the final day's journey they
were constantly in its neighborhood. It was as if Rome
dwelt like a thundercloud on the upper right, menacing
even in its quiescence.

But the crying of the women?

After he had been in his own villa for two or three
hours, had rested, partaken of refreshment and a bath,
Seneca asked.

"Boy," he said to a young Italian slave who was standing
by the marble door which led to the atrium, "boy, do you
know why the women are weeping so loudly?"

"Yes, Lord," the boy said submissively, without lifting
his eyes. He was a recent acquisition and Seneca really did
not know him; he came from somewhere in the Alps as a

result of some military foray or other. The old man looked at him shrewdly. Poor boy. He would never see his native village again. What a dreadful institution, really, what an appalling institution was this of human slavery—! The old man's breath grew short and his eyes drooped.

"If you know what causes the weeping, boy, please tell me," Seneca said. He was not peremptory; at this moment his sympathy for the sad young boy stationed in the doorway was greater than his curiosity about the weeping. If he had been able to mitigate—only to mitigate—the institution of slavery he would have done so; this he told himself over and over again as his time wore to an end. The Empire had not permitted.

"The weeping is for our Lady Augusta, the Empress," the boy said without expression.

Seneca was silent, stunned, frozen, numb.

After a very long time, in which the Italian boy probably thought the old man slept, he aroused himself to speak again.

"We have no empress in Rome," he said coldly. "We have an emperor. It is perhaps too much."

The boy's head dipped a little more.

"Yes, Lord," he said, exactly as if he had understood nothing.

Seneca looked at him for a long time and then spoke very dryly, very impersonally indeed, like a schoolmaster, like what he perhaps always had been.

"I have heard what you say," he specified. "You need not repeat it. I have fully understood that somebody, to whom you refer as Our Lady Augusta and our Empress, is the cause of this weeping, this very loud weeping which I have now heard for two and one-half days. May I ask why?"

"Lord, it is Caesar's order," the slave said, raising bewildered eyes toward his master. "Do you wish me to order the women to be still? There is public mourning everywhere."

"Why, why, why?" the old man asked, sitting up for the first time with a glare in his brilliant blue eyes. From his big armchair he looked toward the marble pillars and the slender Cisalpine boy as if he saw something far more decisive beyond them.

"The death, Lord," the slave stammered. "The death—the death of Our Lady Augusta—O, Lord, is it possible you did not know?"

Seneca put both his long, thin hands over his brow and eyes. He sat thus for a period during which countless pictures flickered and went, superimposed one upon the other, years to remember, years to regret. At last he took down his scrawny hands and put them firmly in his lap and raised his head.

"You may go now, boy," he said steadily. "I regret that I do not know your name."

"It is Lucius, Lord."

"Very well, Lucius. I shall set you free as soon as I can obtain and sign the document. You may return to your Alpine village and remember an old man. Will you send me the major-domo and tell him I have released you from your service this afternoon?"

The Master of the Household, a very old man of mixed ancestry (some said he was part barbarian and part Greek), came in a few minutes later. He was the sort of fellow with whom Seneca had no embarrassments. In fact, this Diogenes had served the family in Spain before Seneca had ever seen

Rome. Granada was perhaps his birthplace—that or Tarragona. He was wrinkled, doddering, ferociously devoted to the family and to Seneca in particular, and, above all, unwilling to recognize that he had been set free quite legally and irreversibly some twenty-five years before.

"Diogenes," Seneca said, "I have just been informed of something I can scarcely believe. The slave boy who was on duty here told me that the weeping I hear, the loud and incessant weeping of the women, is for the death of Caesar's wife."

"That is the truth, Lord."

"When I say Caesar's wife I mean the Lady Poppaea."

"Yes, Lord."

"She is dead?"

"Yes, Lord."

Seneca paused and looked beyond the trembling old man.

"When?" he asked.

"We think two days ago, Lord."

"It is very strange," Seneca said to himself. "How could it be? I do not, I do not—"

He turned directly on the old Master of the Household.

"Diogenes," he said, "you are older than I am, tell me by your faith, how did this happen? The lady to whom they refer is young. That is, she is far younger than we are. By many decades. She had an immensely long time to live. How could she die so suddenly, when she was in such perfect health and spirits? And when everything in this world was combined in her favor?"

"I don't know, Lord," Diogenes said, his voice itself trembling by now. "I can tell you what they say among the people. They say that Caesar kicked her in the belly."

"When she was pregnant?" Seneca breathed forth, more in wonder than in surprise. "But he *wanted* a son, it was the only thing on earth he really wanted—!"

"He came home late the other night," the ancient Major Domo said with eager earnestness. "He had been at the circus, you know. She reproved him because the dinner was spoiled, the banquet, you know. He still had his boots on and he kicked—perhaps in the manner of Hercules in a tragedy—I don't know—and there it was. She was carried out howling, and some hours later, well, you know. And the child, too. And the Emperor is gone wild with grief and sorrow and guilt, you know."

"Yes," said Seneca, "I know."

Paulina came into the room and gently touched the old Diogenes on the wrist as she walked around him.

"Thank you, old friend," Seneca said to the antique figure. To Paulina he said directly: "You should have told me. How long have you known?"

"I have know for two days," she said quietly. "My principal thought was to get you here in good health and give you a little rest. I had intended to tell you now, actually, just now."

"It is only now that I have learned," he said somberly. "Ah, what stars have set, what realms have perished—! Paulina, have you always hated Poppaea?"

"Always," she said. "Always. To me she was the absolute in evil."

"Why?"

"I don't know. It was so. For years it has been true. At the sight of her, at the very sight of her, I wanted to go home. This was when we were everything and she was nothing. Always, always, always."

"The 'empress,' she is called by the slaves. And her effigy is on the coinage. How she has defamed and degraded the Romans! Cornelia, the mother of the Gracchi . . ."

He shaded his eyes with his hand.

"Caesar must turn to you," Paulina said vehemently. "The poor insane boy has nobody else. You are the hope of the Empire. The whole world depends upon you. Poppaea has satiated her cruelty and greed and her love of torture. Nero is afraid of his own shadow. If it were not for the fact that he believes himself to be a great poet and singer, he would commit suicide tonight. The one and only person in this world who can save him is you. Annaeus, you."

"Yes," he said quietly. "One will come from Caesar who will invite me to open my veins. If it is not now, it will be within an hour or so, and if it is not this evening it will be tomorrow."

"How can you say it?" she asked vehemently. "How can you believe such things? The woman is dead. It is she who hated you. The boy has nobody but you."

"Believe me," Seneca said with the utmost tranquillity, "there is nobody on earth whom the world's master hates as he does me. Principally, and quite simply, it is because he would like to take my wealth, which I have always thought was too great. I offered it to him, all of it. He would not take it. He would not take it from me living, but he will take it from me dead."

"It is not sufficient reason," she said. "There are many men of great wealth in the Empire."

"These men of great wealth did not bring him up from the age of eleven, as I did," the old man remarked. "The mere fact that I taught him everything he knows is enough to make him hate me. Wherever he goes, whatever he does, he is reminded of me. He believes that this condition may be changed by my death. He does not realize that I may dwell even more incessantly in his mind when I am no longer here."

"Annaeus," she said, weeping gently, "I do not believe all this. I cannot think the Emperor has such thoughts of you. He could scarcely have existed as a thinking and percipient human being if you had not taught him the very rudiments of life."

"This is the root of the matter," the old man said. "It has been too long, too much, too difficult. He may never understand. He may understand only at the hour of his death. At present he is consumed with hatred of me. It is he who caused the death of his Lady Poppaea—I have only now heard of it—and yet I am certain that in the depths of his clouded soul he holds me responsible. I know that he holds me responsible for anything that happens if it is not conducive to his pleasure."

She wept silently. The old man put his hands over his eyes and fell into a profound abstraction.

A slave came into the room and, finding them thus, went out again.

Seneca aroused himself finally.

"I have written eight tragedies," he said. "Sometimes I have thought their language not unsuited to their theses. I believe that my *Medea* and my *Electra* are within the highest ranges of the Latin language, although not to be compared with the Greek originals. I have even thought fairly highly of my *Oedipus*, in its time. I had a feeling for tragedy. If we had had a really good tragic theater I might even have written some original plays for it. But of course we have no such thing in Rome. My plays have served only for private readings, private declamations, the sort of thing Caesar liked when he was younger and less corrupted by vice. Many times he declaimed my *Medea*. I doubt if he understood a single word."

The old man paused and looked long at Paulina.

"Wife," he said, "these antique tragedies I have composed in my hours of somber thought, remembering ages past—these ancient tragedies I have put in modern words—were they in any way worse than what befalls me?"

Her tears began again and she put her hand out toward him.

"Mine is no less complete, no less inevitable," he said, and then in an undertone: "Although perhaps less beautiful."

"It is not said, it is not done, until it is said and done."

"Paulina, it is the same. It is hubris and it is *até*. What right had I to think that I could create the philosopher-king? If Plato could not, how could I? The opportunity was offered. I tried. But there is no philosopher-king. Those who govern cannot think and those who think cannot govern. It is the world."

"It was not your fault that the most unspeakable monster of all humanity was given you as your instrument, Annaeus, the product of an evil breed, the heir to things beyond your knowledge or control—"

"And so I tell myself over and over, but should I not have known it to begin with? What precept or experience empowered me to attempt that which can never be? Wisdom, virtue, honor, such things cannot be taught. From afar, from a very great distance in time and space, there may come some glimmer of light, some hint of truth. Its source cannot know. The perceiver cannot know. It happens. What I have interposed is the human attempt to act as God, to make a man."

"I do not understand what you are saying, Annaeus, but if you are referring to the Emperor, I should say that nothing could possibly have made him other than a monster. He is no man and he is no woman and he is no prince. His parents, grandparents, all his dreadful family made him. They made him. You did not."

"No," Seneca answered slowly, "no, I cannot say that I did. What I was trying to do was in almost every respect the obverse of what we see. But it was insane pride, intellectual pride, the worst pride of all, that made me even try. I thought I could succeed where Plato failed—where, in fact, everybody has failed. And where, at last, I surrender and die."

"You cannot say it, you must not say it!"

"You will be steady, strong and true, Paulina," he said gently. It was a more personal tone than he had been used to use in these last years. "It will not be easy for you. One will come from Rome—"

"No!" she said.

"One will come from Rome to say that Caesar grants me the privilege of taking my own life. I will open my veins in the bath. There will be no time to write or even to say those last words which the philosopher often looks upon as his possible bequest to the future, the words which will sustain the memory of his passage here. There will be no such time permitted. You will live, and you will write to Lucilius and send him my last epistles."

"No," she said vehemently, "no, I will not live! If you open your veins I will open mine!"

"You cannot do so because it is against the law," he said. "That one who comes from Rome and may now be at the gate will have soldiers with him. He will be an equestrian, a knight, perhaps a centurion. There will be no choice for you or for me. I shall go, but you must remember."

"Annaeus," she said submissively, tears already shed and head already bowed, "I will do what you tell me to do. It is difficult to be a woman."

"Yes, Paulina," he said. "It is also difficult to be a man. I have tried and failed. And all my tragedies have come to one, myself alone."

"I thought you knew," she said, a little bit wildly because her head was going around through the fear he had evoked. "I thought you knew what it was, I mean that it was this or it was that, and it was thus and it was so. I never knew."

"Nor did I," he said.

"Annaeus," she said.

"Paulina," he said.

In the marble arch there appeared the figure of the ancient major-domo, Diogenes, whom some supposed to be Greek and some supposed to be barbarian, a mighty heritage indeed but not Roman, and he was trembling, and both his eyes and his voice were filled with the tears of a lifetime—the lifetime of the slave, of the slave, of the slave, who cannot even know when he has been set free, but must be slave forever.

"Lord," he said, shaking.

Seneca knew at once and took Paulina's hand in both of his.

"Wife, lady and friend," he said to her, "it was my ultimate or original instructor, Zeno, who said: *The wise man will always intervene in the affairs of the state if circumstance does not deter him.* And yet it is perfectly true, and you may tell Lucilius after it is all over, that I now think that ancient Epicurus, to whom Zeno made reply, was more right. What he said was: *The wise man will always hold himself afar from state affairs if circumstance does not drag him into them by force.*"

Paulina moaned faintly and clung to his hand.

"I do not really know the difference," she said almost in a whisper.

"Perhaps there is none," he said, "none at all."

After a moment the old man raised his commanding head and demanded: "Diogenes, what do you want?"

The ancient trembled and wept. At last he said: "Lord, one has come from Rome."

About the Author

VINCENT SHEEAN has become a legend during his own lifetime. Forty years of world history are embedded in his amazing journalistic career, which has often made him a behind-the-scenes witness of grave social and political change. Within this period he has produced more than twenty volumes, many of which have reflected his keen insights concerning such events. Among these are *Personal History, Not Peace But a Sword, Lead, Kindly Light: Gandhi and the Way to Peace,* and *Nehru: The Years of Power.* Others have revealed his personal attitudes toward music—*First and Last Love* and *Orpheus at Eighty* (a biography of Verdi). Between times he has written several novels based on themes and people observed by a cosmopolite. Most recently, he did a biography of two old friends, Sinclair Lewis and Dorothy Thompson, under the title *Dorothy and Red.* As a student of history, Mr. Sheean has always taken the long view of human affairs. His current novel, set in imperial Rome, mingles ancient lore with a superb working knowledge of intrigue in power politics.